Novels of Driss Chraibi by Three Continents from

The Berber Tetralogy:

1. *The Flutes of Death (Une Enquête au pays)*, translated by Robin Roosevelt
2. *Mother Spring (La Mère du Printemp)*, translated by Hugh Harter
3. *Birth at Dawn (Le Naissance à l'aube)*, translated by Ann Woollcombe

Other Chraibi Titles:

The Simple Past (Le Passé Simple), translated by Hugh Harter
The Butts (Les Boucs), translated by Hugh Harter
Mother Comes of Age (La Civilisation, ma mère!), translated by Hugh Harter

BIRTH AT DAWN

DRISS CHRAIBI

Translated by Ann Woollcombe

An Original By Three Continents

Copyright © Ann Woollcombe 1990

A Three Continents Book

Published in the United States of America by
Lynne Rienner Publishers, Inc.
1800 30th Street, Boulder, Colorado 80301

© by Three Continents of Cover Art
by Max K. Winkler

Library of Congress Cataloging-in-Publication Data

Chraibi, Driss, 1926–
[Naissance à l'aube. English]
Birth at dawn / Driss Chraibi ; translated from the French by
Ann Woollcombe. 1st English language ed.
p.   cm.
Translation of: Naissance à l'aube.
ISBN 0-89410-576-0 (cloth) : $22.00 —
ISBN 0-89410-577-9 (pbk.) : $10.00
I. Title.
PQ3989.C5N3513   1990   86-51006
843—dc20   CIP

© 1986, Editions du Seuil

I dedicate this book to my native land, Morocco and to the Moroccan people, my people.

D.C.

From water, we have created
all living things
Koran

In the year of grace nineteen hundred and eighty-five, Raho Aït Yafelman walked along the road on a bright summer morning. He was a Berber, very tall and very thin with a serene face. He did not walk on the tarred road, but on the shoulder where for years his own steps had trodden down the grass and the gravel until the lane was as hard as granite. The soles of his feet were as thick as a bicycle tire and his slippers were safe in the hood of his djellaba, together with a piece of barley bread and some dates. He would put on his shoes when he entered the city so he would be properly dressed. From here to there he had only a three-hour walk ahead of him, perhaps four. But it was the month of August, the air stood still or rather, there wasn't any. It was as if ever since dawn the sun had sent its flames up to the seventh heaven.

1

Here and there, the steaming tar shone, had turned to liquid. The road was twisted into mad curves for no apparent reason, breaking the rhythm of his strides. But that is the way it was: one had to march with one's century! Setting one foot in front of the other, one after the other, the man from the mountain calmly made his way, going down to the city of Sidi Kacem Bou Asriya and at the same time back into his past. Across space, over there to the left, very far south, was the Oum-er-Bia. Not a day went by that Raho did not think of the river of his youth, torrential at its source, peaceful where it joined the sea, heavy, slow and deep in its flow. Had he ever left its banks? Still now, at the threshold of old age, he heard the voice of its waters pour forth like an organ, from the Atlas mountains to the Atlantic ocean.

Every time he took a step, every time his body moved, the little bells and coins that covered him, chimed gaily. They were at his wrists, on the tassels of his chechia, on his shoulders and all over the water bag, made of a goat's udder, he carried around his neck on a strap. He would fill his water bag with nice cool water, at noon, at the train station, in the office of Mr. Boursexe. Then he would go from train to train ministering to the travelers' thirst during the noon day heat. He asked for nothing in exchange. Never would the thought have struck his mind to get paid: like the light of the skies the water belonged to everybody. He held his full cup out to the thirsty, red-faced and sweaty people, simply saying:

"Here brother! (or: here, uncle! sister, little mother, or "mista" or "pretty lady" when they were Christians.) Drink and may peace be with you!"

If someone held on to his sleeve and put a coin into his hand, or maybe even a banknote, but that was an exception, well then, he accepted it quietly. It was the custom, perhaps also a show of brotherhood between men when they were thirsty, when they were suffering, or when they were alone with their heart. Yes, perhaps that was it . . .

What he was sure of, and for a long time already, was that mista Boursexe was a brother. A real brother in the spirit of the clan, even if he was born in the land of the Franks and belonged to the class of the masters and the sedentary people. He was . . . let's see now! Oh yes, a cooperant, that's what he was. He ran the train station. Many employees. He commanded the trains, the rails, even the minutes of time. Therefore he must have brains, even though his head was not swollen like a king's. In a corner of his office there was a sort of large white bowl fastened to the wall, a sink it was called, and out of its faucet appeared water that was miraculously cool, summer like winter. It had nothing in common with that other faucet on the platform, standing up straight like a hammer at the end of a long hose as thick as a log, in the full sun. First of all, when they wanted to touch it, the railroad workers had to wear old gloves or use wadded-up paper. And, if they had managed to turn the faucet on, they had to jump back and wait for almost a quarter of an hour until the steam had evaporated and turned into water to fill the trains' reservoirs.

There were three trains: one came from the south and went north; the other travelled in the opposite direction; and the third originated in the country of the Algerians and its terminus was Bar el Beïda, Casablanca. Hundreds of meters long they were, all three of them, from the first to the fourth class, without counting the freight cars, the postal vans and the animal transports. Their meeting point (the railway junction, as mista Boursexe had explained to Raho Aït Yafelman time and time again during these last few years) was here, in Sidi Kacem Bou Asriya, in the geographical centre of the country. Easy, no?

"No," answered Raho. Oh no, mista Boursexe. You have brains. There are a lot of things in them, *wallah*. But why do the three trains arrive at the same time in the middle of the day? Hey, you? You explain to this Berber? It is hot between noon and one o'clock in the afternoon, isn't it? What are your brains good for? Why don't you make your trains arrive in the morning, or at night, when the sun is not like fire? The travellers are out there, roasting like a goat on the spit. They are not like the rest of us, the Sons of the Land. The heat makes them suffer before they even go to hell. And why don't you tell the drivers of the trains, all right, they stopped to rest a little, fine. But that's enough now and they should get on their way. What are you waiting for?"

"I am waiting for the train from Tangier. Get out of here! *Roh, fissa!* Let me get my work done!"

"You get angry fast, you. Tangier, that's far away, up there in the North. By the time the train from Tangier will arrive! . . . The soup in the pot will have dried up, no more soup at all. And you, mista Boursexe, you are there scribbling with a pencil. I not understand you."

"Listen here," the station chief said with great kindness. (He was very hurt.) A train needs a rail. The two which are at the platform can not leave until the train from Tangier arrives. It's a matter of switching rails. They are trains, not camels or mules who can go whichever way they please and where they please, even to the devil. Trains use rails and there are only two, one to the right and one to the left. Two sets of rails, iron paths, if you prefer. You understand?"

"I understand you, but not your words. The city is in a hole, in a bowl. Around it, there is nothing but hills and plains. There is a lot of heat coming from everywhere, especially in the summer, as you well know. And when it has heated up nicely, it comes down into the city from all sides; it's like the furnace of Gehenna. Say, mista Boursexe, you who have brains, why did you build the station in this place? Don't you like the travellers? Ordinarily you are not mean, *wallah.*"

"Get out of here."

And Raho got out to still the thirst of the sons of Adam and Eve, stuck in their cars and prisoners of civilization—while his grandson Bourguine, this happy wretch with his short legs, round face and squat figure, dressed in a mud-colored djellaba which came down to his knees, hopped from train to train. He swung the postal bags the baggage handlers (you could only see their arms, the rest of their body was invisible in summer) held out to him, over his shoulder, piled them on a hand cart with iron-clad wheels, placed himself inside the shafts, pulled or pushed the cart suiting his fancy, hopping along the trains on his bare feet, singing at the top of his lungs some tribes-men songs which made the hair of the Moroccans stand up on end. He crossed the rails, lost his cargo en route, picked it up as fast as he could and balanced it more or less on the cart which he dumped on platform B like a truckload of sand. He rubbed his hands, arrived at the height of the postal car of the second train, hammered on the door and yelled as if he were standing on a mountain top in the Atlas:

"Are you going to open up, you? Are you constipated? Are you going to bring out your miserable mail bags?"

And he flew in the other direction, along platform B, crossed the rails and ran along the second convoy, from its tail to its head, calling to the *moul bousta*, the post master, mista Georges:

"Hey, chief! Mission accomplished. Are you happy with me?"

Mr. Georges, the warehouse man, stood on the threshold of the hangar, one meter ninety tall and his hundred kilos of muscle dripping with sweat, he was wearing shorts and a T-shirt. Within easy reach a case of beer rested on three or four other cases. Half of the beer cans were already empty.

"He, mista Georges!" said Bourguine. "You are drinking quite a lot, say. You will be confused in the head in a little while and you won't be able to do the work of the administration. You are the chief, not I."

Even though his face was congested and his eyes blood-shot, Mr. Georges did not lose his cool nor his official dignity. Slowly he removed his glasses and wiped them with his thumb to clean off the fog. He put them back on his nose and his leaden look fell upon this Berber phenomenon who laughed with all his thirty-two teeth.

"Where is the mail?" he asked slowly in a hoarse whisper.

"Here," answered Bourguine with great simplicity. "And the other is over there. There is nothing to worry about, one coming from the south, well, that's the train that will climb up there; the one coming from the north, that will go down. I can not make a mistake, the locomotives don't look at each other. One faces here, the other down there, in the opposite direction. I understood everything. I've quickly done the work like I should, no need to explain things to me twice."

"You did it on purpose?" exclaimed Mr. Georges. (His voice had risen by a decibel.)

"Oh no, chief. I am like that. Everybody knows me. Ask Grandfather Raho. He is mista Boursexe's friend. He says I am clever, quick and all that."

"And the third train?"

"What third train? It hasn't come yet, I don't see it. And maybe it won't have any mail. Why you worry, mista Georges?"

"And the sorting?" howled Mr. Georges.

At the same time, one locomotive was put under pressure, the other one gave off steam, obliging Mr. Georges to repeat his question at the top of his lungs:

"AND THE SORTING, YOU MULE?"

"Drink one more beer, mista Georges. You losing control . . . The sorting, well, that's simple. The others in the cities will do it in the shade. And if it is all mixed up, there are other trains and other days God made. Tomorrow, or the day after, *incha Allah!* All right, chief?"

"You are fired! *Roh! Fissah!*

"Okay, chief. I am fired. I *roh*. I *fissa*. Pay me for my day. But, tell me, mista Georges, who is going to do my work? In the winter, in the autumn, the flower season, all right. But in the summer, hey, what then? There is not a Christian, not even an Arab or a mule who will go out into this sun. You want to go check?"

"Go and bring the mail bags here. Right here to the hangar and we will sort them."

"I do what you say, mista Georges, but you give little *fabor*, small tip."

"Go and get those bags, you monkey."

"Yes, chief. I go and I get right away. But first you spit on the ground. Then I can be sure there will be little *fabor*. You give whatever you like: small coin, moldy old bill, pack of cigarettes. It's between you and your conscience. And you have a big heart, mista Georges."

The engine had finished blowing off steam, the train from Tangier entered the station and Mr. Georges looked at his watch, spit over the head of the curious boy. He was not really mean. Perhaps a bit too zealous and bossy in his work, but inside he was not the slightest bit mean. It sufficed to talk to him like to a mule without his mate to cool him down a little and get his mind on to something else. At the end of the day, when the sun had crossed the land and put the ocean on fire, Mr. Georges reverted back to what he was, a son of the land and happy to live there. He ate the *kesra*, the traditional bread of the country made by the women, cous-cous, drank mint tea, and enjoyed the cool air on the terrace of a café in the medina in the company of silent Berbers, until nightfall. And, then, he liked to play poker. Sometimes Bourguine let him win.

"My grandson is an infidel," Raho told himself as he went down the aisles of the car, going from one compartment to the next, from thirsty traveller to thirsty traveller, offering his cup of fresh water and his comforting words:

"Drink, brother. And may peace be with you. What tribe do you belong to? Aha, the Bani Mellil? You grow grain crops in your area, don't you? . . .

"Today's youth has many thorns," he thought. "And Bourguine has not yet twenty summers. Eighteen, perhaps . . . Seventeen or nineteen summers of time. It's the people of the city and his mercenary spirit. He claims that he says his five daily prayers like a good Muslim. But he doesn't say them at the proper times. He says them all together in the evening, one after the other and in a great hurry before going to sleep. Like that, he is at peace with God and with me. Sometimes, on Sundays, when he is not working, he says all of his prayers for the week ahead. He is an infidel born of my loins. I can recite him all the suras of the Book as long as I like, he talks to me about oil and good deals. He never stops counting money. He does not know how to purify himself of this century. He envies and at the same time admires all the people who have things, make things and don't amount to anything. Hm, on the other hand, he brings all he can find to the village, flour sacks to make sturdy clothes for the women, shoes he steals from the military, things to eat and drink. Plus his pay. Perhaps he is a decent infidel, after all? . . . "

The trains were gone, the platforms deserted, the door of the hangar padlocked behind Mr. Georges, and all that remained in the whole area of the station were the shiny rails, the hand cart with its shafts pointing to the brilliant sky and an old man, surrounded by the chimes of brass and copper at every step he took. He stopped and, standing straight under the scorching sun, turned slowly, not a drop of sweat on his face. Heat was a gift, just like the rain when it fell from the sky, the bitter wind in the winter or the burning wind loaded with red sand coming from the South, all these disorders, except those caused by man. The clock showed one, but Raho did not trust these machines that divided time. Turning around he saw that his body left no shadow. So it must be time for the second prayer of the day, the noon day prayer.

"In the name of the all-merciful God," he recited, entering the office of Mr. Boursexe. "In the middle of the day. And at night."

With his right hand he shielded his face so he would not see what the station chief was eating. A *hanouf* sandwich! Pork! He seized a broom, swept a corner of the room, pressed his water bag to perform his ablutions and, with the few drops left over, he sprinkled the floor as if he were sprinkling it with holy water. And then, quietly, he took off his slippers, his djellaba, took the time table of the trains off the wall and removed the poster of the Christian who displayed her sun-tanned pears, the shameless hussy! . . . everything on the east wall facing Mecca. Having finished his prayers, he put the thumb tacks back into the wall. Everything was put back exactly as it had been, even the blonde with her ripe fruit—but he had turned her to the wall.

"Don't you like women?" Mr. Boursexe had asked him one day.

"Oh yes, mista, a lot, a lot, but not during prayer."

"One would say you are ashamed."

"Oh no, mista. There is no shame in me. I don't wear underpants like you do. You are the one who's ashamed."

"What do you mean, I am ashamed? But I adore women, the pretty ones, of course. It's terrible."

"I am not saying the contrary. But why do you put them on the wall instead of in your bed? You work more with your brains than with your nuts, don't you?"

Mr. Boursexe's laughter rose, instinctive, free and pure, like the laughter of a small child whose mother offers him her breasts, heavy with milk, when he wakes up. Raho's laughter, coming from the bottom of his heart, joined in. And while the station chief's kettle hummed on the spirit cooker in preparation for the tea and the old man from the mountain was munching a mouth-full of barley bread followed by a date (he put the pits in the pocket of his djellaba), the two men talked about their respective countries. They "traded." Mr. Boursexe came from the Limousin.

"By Allah and the Prophet, but you are a Berber like me."

"How is that?"

"There are cousins in the High Atlas, the Aït Limoussen. They are the same as you. Perhaps they come from your village? Or the other way around? Try and figure it out with History coming and going! Seems like us a long time ago, we were the masters in your place. For a long, long time. So of course, we are related by blood. You don't have to worry about the women when they smell two or three Berbers around. They are the ones who have the little ones . . . and make History. Aït Limousin! (He hugged Mr. Boursexe.) You are a Chleuh, a Moroccan tribesman, my brother! It's those political scribblers who gave you a name like that, Boursexe. One just has to look at your round head and your sly little eyes, just like the fellows from around here. Is that the reason, tell me, that you are always asking me about the birds of the mountains? You don't eat them, you don't even own a gun, yet you keep asking me questions about these sky dwellers. Tell me about the Aït Limousin, my cousins from across the sea . . ."

This had been going on for years. Ever since Mr. Boursexe had become station chief of Sidi Kacem Bou Asriya and on that day in July long ago, he had allowed Raho to fill his water bag under the faucet of the sink. As the months and the seasons passed, not a friendship, but a Berber brotherhood, was born between them.

Raho knew that no matter how true and how profound a friendship was (just like a love), it was at the mercy of feelings. And feelings could change, mature, get old and die in the space of a spring or a lifetime. He did not tell Mr. Boursexe—because he did not know the words to do so—that Christianity in the beginning signified before anything else the love of one's neighbor such as he was, in the flesh if not in his soul, and that the original Islam proposed the "Oumma," the human community where all tribes and races on this earth were equal. Both religions spoke in the name of an immense caïd who lived up there in heaven. But his orders had not been followed. Muslims and Nazarenes had spent the better part of the centuries to kill one another. Then, they joined forces and attacked those who had never heard of this terrible and invisible caïd, devastating the land and its sons, men, trees and animals. They called that "civilization."

If Raho was a Muslim, it was in good faith. The most peaceful in the world, he was very sincere and had not the slightest wish for power. Without fail, he said his five daily prayers, fasted during the month of Ramadan, gave the "zaka" to those poorer than he, proscribed from his table and his sight all that was forbidden by divine law and often remained tongue in cheek in order not to tell a lie or utter a hurtful word. Thus he remained what his ancestors had been from the beginning of time, a Berber from ancient times, from the depths of his heart to the marrow of his sex. A very long time ago, before History was written down, there had been the oath of the first Ancients sworn in the quick waters of the Oum-er-Bia. Ever since then, generations of Berbers had pronounced this oath, word for word, emotion for emotion, like on that bright spring morning in the year 679 according to Christ, son of Meryem. When Raho had to swear the oath when he was nine or ten years old, the day his member became virile, his mother had explained the battle of time to him, speaking in the thousand-years old words of the tribe: Perpetuate the race, survive the invaders by procreating the largest number of descendants possible, both male and female. Submerge, drown all the masters in seas of blood. And time had passed and been generous to the Sons of the Land. Only one or two centuries to wait. . . . Soon, the past would rise again and outdistance the future . . .

Raho Aït Yafelman tried to figure in his old head while he laughed and talked with Mr. Boursexe. Let's see! How many sons, daughters and grandchildren had sprung from his loins since his long ago puberty to this afternoon in August of the year nineteen eighty-five? Oh, almost the whole village. Drought, famine and politics had only killed three or four, perhaps. Crab grass grows in good and in bad years, with thorny roots as deep as a well.

"How many do you have?"

"What? asked the station chief, what are you talking about?"

"Children. How many have you got? "

"Just one. A boy."

"You work too much with your head. Mustn't put the women on the wall, have to put them in your bed. Paper women are not much use, no juice, no heat, no little ones. Go ahead, cousin, tell me about your village."

It was difficult to express, even with the words of his childhood. But he knew deep down that the Berber brotherhood, the essence of liberty and the essence of good luck was worth more than anything else on earth, and the brotherhood born between him and this Aït Limoussen made them forever equals, because it was based not on an ideology, but on what had preceded man and would always survive him: the land. And men were the sons of the land before being the sons of their ideas.

"Go ahead, Aït Limoussen! Speak to me of your village. You are not born in this noisy train station? You do have a shack where you come from? . . . Talk!"

Asking questions with the persistence that is usually allowed only children, he asked precise, unexpected questions. No, no, Limoges china did not interest him, but not at all. He had no need for plates or for cups. Furthermore, he had nothing to put in them. He was not interested in towns, either, which when all is said and done, are nothing but stones collected and put up by men to protect themselves against the elements and against loneliness. What he wanted was to discover the natives of the Limousin through the power of the living language. Imagination and emotion would do the rest.

"Tell me about the land at your place. Is there any sun?"

"A little. Not much. Nothing to compare to this furnace."

"I see. That's why you are so pale. Are there trees?"

"Yes. Walnut and chestnut trees."

"Men and trees walk together, but not at the same pace."

"You know, my province is rather poor."

"Is that why you came here, to this land of milk and honey? You did not get very rich, did you? Neither did I. Any *oueds*?"

"Rivers? Oh yes, of course. There is the Vienne, the Creuse, the Corrèze and the Vézère which goes through the village I was born in. It is not a big river, about 190 kilometers, like from here to Casablanca."

"I don't know that Casablanca. It's far away. Talk about your village which is closer to me."

"What do you want to know?"

"Everything, mista Boursexe: its beginning, its end, its whole life. Its history."

"Well then. It's source is in the high plane of the Millevaches" (literally translated 'thousand cows') . . .

"Oh! *wallah!* there is enough to eat then for the whole tribe till the end of all famines and for a long time thereafter. A thousand cows, you can't be serious! I no understand you: you leave the cows in the village and you scribble here at the train station with train puzzles."

Mr. Boursexe's laughter, about forty years old, cascaded from memory to memory until it reached the present. The next train was not due until late in the afternoon. Until then, it felt good to go back to the beginning of his childhood.

"But no," he explained to the old mountaineer sitting cross-legged on the floor between two chairs, slowly sipping his mint tea. "They are not cows with horns and a tail, moo, moo! It is old French and the word 'vache' used to mean 'source'."

Raho balanced his glass on his knee, Berber-fashion.

"Wait a minute, you! Be patient! Did you say . . . you did say a thousand springs? A thousand? Ten times ten, hundred multiplied by ten, that makes an even thousand? But that is abundance? There is nothing . . . you understand, nothing at all that is more life-giving than water."

"I know that. But where I come from, it is not a baraka. Quite the opposite."

"The masters took the best fields, just like over here? It doesn't matter, brother. They will die. They make love to money, to worldly goods, they don't beget children. They will die, I tell you. In three centuries or in three thousand years, that's not very long. And the land will come back to the Aït Limoussen, fattened with the corpses of the masters. There! Have some tea in the meantime. Tell about the mountains, the paths, the clouds."

"There are prehistoric caves, the caves of Lascaux. There are wall paintings, dating from the end of the Solutrian era to the beginning of the Magdalenian."

"Is that a Berber dialect from your country that you talk? Ah, *wallah!* The French have obliterated the memory of my cousins . . . I don't understand a word of that language. 'Maglanlinane . . . solulallah' . . . nothing at all, mista Boursexe."

Mr. Boursexe choked with laughter and Raho hit him on the back, asking worriedly:

"You are not going to die right away, say, brother? Wait a little. You have not finished your story. Tell it first before you go to join your Maker!"

After a while, having calmed down, sitting once more on the chair from which he had fallen while laughing, the station chief explained with very simple words and quite seriously that the Magdalenian and the Solutrian eras . . . "no, I am not going to repeat . . . went way back in History, fifteen centuries before Christ . . . that's right! Issa the son of Meryem as you call him, no I don't think he too was a Berber will you let me talk for Christ's sake? . . . What Aït Krouman? The man of Cro-Magnon, I tell you, your ancestor, if you like . . . get out of here, I have had it . . . come back tomorrow . . ."

Mr. Boursexe adored birds, adored them with a passion. Not because of their beauty, not even because of their singing. He adored them because of their freedom. Those who were rare, who fled from humans, those whose species were about to be extinct. The black Ibis, the red-billed ravens, the bearded vultures who, when they stood up were as tall as a man and whose wing-span was as wide as a sailboat. Raho told him about the home of these birds, his home: the mountain villages of Timhadit and Bekrit, the djebel Roumyat, the high cliffs from which sprang the source of the Oum-er-Bia. With Raho's words, poetry reached its full dimension: the innermost feelings expressed in full, concrete, pantheistic words. Year after year, listening to the words of the barefoot water carrier, who knew nothing about books and those who wrote them, Mr. Boursexe discovered with a mixture of awe and joy that the human spirit was used to being spoon-fed with the thoughts of others, but that sometimes in solitude found and accepted, this nourishment was withheld. At that point, man began to think for himself.

From now on, he spent his vacations, not in France which he had always loved (one's country is, before anything else, one's childhood; one can renounce everything, except one's childhood), but in this "other place" which gave his human dimension greater depth and scope: the Atlas. And there he was, a man crouched on the edge of a plateau, far away in time and space, immensely far from the station, the trains and his daily routine; above him, the djebel Roumyat reaching a height of two thousand meters, calcareous rocks, bare of any trees or shrubs, except for some boxwood from which agile squirrels fled like missiles; two wild sheep pursued each other amorously, jumping through the air from rock to rock; the gold, the ochres, the sienna and the amethyst of the rising sun; to the left, across a ravine, a white egg as big as a melon sat on a stump. In a few years, it would become one of the giant vultures filling the skies. And on the bottom of the cliff going straight down, the abyss of a thousand voices. From the loins of the mountain in rut, at the height of its manhood, sprang forth its mighty and roaring semen, a green waterfall, the Mother of Spring, that would fertilize hundreds of kilometers of plains right to the Atlantic Ocean.

The man who was in this symphony of life, in the midst of this continuing birth, had long since forgotten, lost his name. But he found what had existed before that name, before all the words created by convention: his identity. The power not to be fighting the land that had nursed him any longer, nor himself . . .

"Pa," said Bourguine.

He had not opened his mouth since they passed the village of Tselfat. He had needed an hours' march, perhaps two, to weigh his words. He too walked barefoot along the road, but on the other shoulder, the tarred road between his grandfather and himself like a respectful distance due the elder generation.

"Hey?" Raho asked.

Both slowed down, stopped. Then they faced each other, speaking in the loud voices of mountaineers. The sky was white above them. Around them, as far as the eye could reach, the ground was parched from the endless August sun. Down below, or even farther down, they could see some green oases flecked with orange, surrounded by living fences or barbed wire, but they were the private property of others—thus they were not really part of the landscape. They showed off their riches like an insult to the poverty of the Sons of the Land. That is why Raho and his grandson would not acknowledge what they saw with their own eyes. This was another world. For them, it did not exist.

"Pa!" Bourguine yelled at the top of his lungs. "The town has become the town again."

He paused, thought for a minute before he dared make a personal comment:

"At least, that's what it looks like."

"What?" Raho asked, cupping his hand over his ear as if he had not heard properly.

"Yes. Before the town was called Sidi Kacem Bou Asriya, after the saint who had lived there. And then, the Nazarenes came, this was before I was born. They pacified the tribes and lost a cap'n. Unless it was a serg'n, I don't know too well. Any case, one of their soldier brothers they buried right there with a big stone block on top of him. Petitjean he was called, the fellow. So, of course, they called the town Petitjean, after the old corpse. Now that they have left, since everything is peaceful, in order and the way it should be, well, the town is once more Sidi Kacem Bou Asriya, like in the old days."

When he thought some more, he laughed. He could hardly talk for laughing.

"Perhaps . . . perhaps they . . . perhaps they took along . . . the moldy old corpse of the man, what do you think, Pa?"

Raho let him laugh. When he saw his grandson close his mouth, he said:

"I don't know this town. Not by one name, nor by the other. All this . . . (he slowly turned on his heels, his arm outstretched. he pointed to the horizons, the East and the West, the whole radius of the world) . . . here and here, and there and there and then down there, everything belongs to the tribe of the Cherarda, our brothers and cousins. Of course, all they have are thistles and stones, but this is their territory since the beginning of creation and until the end of the centuries. Son, you can see no farther than your eyesight allows. You have to look at time."

"Yes, Pa."

"They continued their march, walked two or three kilometers. Bourguine hung his head and seemed to count the tufts of dry grass under his feet. The old man from the mountains walked quietly, his body upright, looking straight ahead of him. And then, they stopped almost in the same second, as if they had communicated through telepathy. Raho said:

"Thirty-seven nickels average per day in the four-and-a-half months of summer, 5 during the two winter months, 14 the rest of the year, 13 bills worth ten pieces each, and 2.5 per cent of that sum is how much?"

"That makes 222 pieces and one copper which is worth half a nickel," Bourguine answered at once and without hesitating in the slightest. "In our lunar year, of course. For the year of the Nazarenes, which has five days more when it is normal and six when it is twisted, well, that's easy: that makes you a round sum of 225 pieces."

Raho blew smoke through his nostrils. He said:

"I am not a Nazarene."

"No, Pa. I calculated like they do, that's all."

"I am born in my country and I live in my country."

"So am I, Pa. So you have 222 nickels and one copper piece. The Nazarenes have banknotes, am I stupid! Coins, that's for the rest of us. When there are any. And that has hardly changed with the government of Independence."

"You talk too much. Needlessly."

"Yes, Pa. I don't have your wisdom yet, I am not married yet so I can play the man with a woman instead of playing with words."

Bumper to bumper, four trucks passed between them, groaning, heavily laboring uphill. They did not even glance at the trucks. And yet, those trucks were loaded with the most beautiful oranges in the country, blood oranges, Washingtons and "Ouezzanes". A long time later, the looked down and saw the tire tracks in the soft tarred surface. Raho said:

"How can you count faster than the devil, without a pencil and without thinking?"

"Poker, Pa!" Bourguine answered and started to laugh.

"Don't laugh, Bourguine."

"No, Pa."

"You are an infidel. God's religion formally forbids all games of chance."

"Yes, Pa, absolutely. But with me, it is not chance. I don't know what comes over me as soon as I touch a pack of cards. It's the others who trust to chance, since they lose three quarters of the time . . . not to say always."

"Son of my son, you are a thief."

"Oh, no, Pa. You mustn't think that. They know nothing about poker, like others know nothing about our country. So I take advantage of their ignorance to help the needy of the village."

Enough time passed to boil an egg or to unravel a thought. Then Raho said:

"Today the *zaka* is due, the penny for the poor. Of all a Muslim earns in a year he must, according to God's law, give two -and -a -half per cent to the poor. More if he is rich. It's between a man and his conscience. THE MONEY HAS TO BE PURIFIED."

Bourguine rolled the whites of his eyes. He did not understand and said:

"But Pa, we are all poor . . . "

"No," Raho cut him off. "There are always those who are poorer than we are. Don't go "carding" or "pokering" with God's commandments. As for me, I have put away, day after day, 211 pieces for the *zaka*. In a little while, *incha Allah*, I will earn 37 others, a little more, a little less. Perhaps the 12 nickels missing from the total. And you . . . (He pointed an accusing finger at his grandson) . . . you will do the same."

"But Pa, I spent it all, I have . . . "

"Do as you like, wash your soul, wring it out and hang it up to dry in the sun. But between now and the evening prayer, you will have to have figured two-and-a-half per cent—and found them—which belong to the poor. All you have earned at the station with your boss mista Georges, and all you have stolen from the idle and rich with your devilish cards. Start walking and figure. You have brains. Don't tell me otherwise."

"All right, Pa. All right."

They stopped a third time, almost at the entrance to the village. This time it was Bourguine who stopped first. Something had been worrying him for the last four or five kilometers. He had had time to mentally play a game of heads or tails—and it was heads. The sun now blazed from the centre of the sky. There was not a soul in the streets. Not even the tail of a dog.

"Pa!" Bourguine said.

"What?" said Raho.

"Pa, I am not going to go to work today. I think the cards will save my soul in an hour or two. Allah is great and merciful. And then, there is no more station."

"What are you telling me? What kind of teeth-pulling lies are these?"

"Well, you see, the train station is still there. But there is no more mista Georges."

"Is he sick?"

"No, Pa. He went back to his country."

"Aha! *wallah?*"

"*Wallah!* I have known since last night. I had trouble falling asleep. It took me almost five minutes. The idiot crushed my hand saying: 'good bye, ground hog'. He has been replaced with a chief from over here. That's politics for you. Up and down like a bucket in a well."

Raho thought in all directions of time and space. Then he said categorically:

"Go to work at the train station, do twice or three times as much of your daily chore so you can get the money together for the *zaka*.

"But Pa . . ."

"The trains and the postal bags are still there. And there is the new boss, a fellow from our own country. He is a brother."

"Yes, Pa. But he does not know me, this brother. He says you have to have papers to load the bags on the cart and take them from one train to the other."

"Papers? What kind of papers?"

"Official ones, Pa. Identity cards, work permits, enough nonsense to make the balls drop from between a man's legs, and the hose with them . . . with all due respect, Pa. That's what it's like, freedom."

The old man from the mountain was confused by this unexpected turn of History. He hoped for the best and rejected the worse in advance. He said:

"Son of my son, one thing after the other. The *zaka* first of all. God first, men after that. Go where your duty calls you, go play cards and fleece the rich, just enough to gather what you owe the poor. Go, Bourguine, and may God help and forgive you."

"Yes, Pa," Bourguine said without enthusiasm.

He danced from one foot to the other. Looking at him in horror, Raho suddenly understood.

"He too?" he asked.

"Yes, Pa."

"Mista Boursexe is gone?"

"Yes, Pa."

Alla Akbar! the descendant of the Oum-er-Bia concluded. God is the greatest.

He felt like dying, yet at the same time he reproached himself vehemently. "Look here! he told himself. It is nothing, nothing at all. From what I see, I am still too young and too inexperienced to feel as I feel. Peace be with you, Raho Aït Yafelman, peace, peace! . . . Brotherhood is not a possession, you know that well. It is like two caravans: two men have met, exchanged what there was to exchange. And then . . . and then, each of them went his way in life. It is fate. Peace with your memories, Son of the Land and the eternal river."

He stood for a moment, like a post on the side of the road, dry, silent and grave, absent from the world and from himself. Suddenly, all the wrinkles of his face began to move, like the alluvium of a delta, giving birth to a flood of joy. He said softly:

"He went back to his tribe, the Aït Limoussen."

"Yes, Pa," Bourguine who felt like crying, agreed. "Surely. And he will have tales to tell till the end of his days."

"In his village, there are many rivers. Four or five, from what he told me."

"Oh yes, Pa. That means more than they need."

"So therefore . . . so therefore, he must not have taken along that white thing he called a 'sink'."

"Oh, no, Pa. You mustn't believe that. There are plenty of sinks in the land of the Franks. One in each shack, sometimes two, from what the brothers who went to work there have told me."

"Aha, is that the truth?"

"Yes, Pa. They are like that, the French. They need several things at once to be happy: two sinks, two countries . . . "

"The new one, you know him?"

"The new station chief? I have not seen him yet. But he is a skinny little fellow in his thirties, with a mustache and wears glasses like a professor. Married, three children, a black car, latest model, a Pijou (Peugeot). The Chleuhs I played cards with last night know nothing about him either, except that he doesn't like poker, his maid's name is Fatima and he comes from the capital, Rabat. His name is Mohammed."

"Then he is a brother," Raho concluded.

"Yes, Pa. You are right."

o o o

Never again would Raho gain entrance to the office of the station chief. Not on that particular day nor on the day of the last judgement. One did not just walk in there. "And what do you want, grandpa? This is not the market place. Get out of here. Roh! Clear out! Go begging where you please, but not here. This is the train station, we are working in this place. Working! What *zaka*? The penny for the poor? Ah yes, religion, tradition . . . Sure it's hot, but what do you expect me to do about it? What sons of Adam and Eve are dying of thirst? I don't understand a word of your gibberish. You are taking what train? No, the one from Algeria has not arrived yet, go to gate C . . . The three trains, you say? Listen, you. I respect old people, but by God, I . . . Where are you going with your bundle? Do you have a platform ticket?"

He lost neither patience nor faith. This man, coming from the Atlantic coast where sometimes a fresh wind blew from the sea, did not yet know Sidi Kacem Bou Asriya. And here it was the middle of August, around noontime. Perhaps it was the first time he had to administer a whole train station under a blazing sun which made his blood boil with big bubbles like those of a soup. Without counting the trains, three of them, which all arrived within the same hour from three different directions and which he had to put on the proper rails. And rails, there were only two of them. No, this well-dressed man from the city was not really angry. His words just ran away with him. He collected his thoughts to face the twentieth century. Perhaps he came from a souk or a medina, where life was not written down on a piece of paper. Yes, that must be it. Tomorrow, or in a season or two he would calm down and become a brother like mista Boursexe. Surely. For the moment, he was only a poor stranger . . .

"May the peace of God put your head in order, son!" Raho told him.

And calmly he left the train station, wound his way around the buildings, slipped between two trains blowing off steam, and with a corner of his djellaba opened the big faucet at the end of the platform. A quarter of an hour later, his water bag filled with lukewarm water, he climbed the steps of the first car he came to, his soul far from any impatience, as if the history of the nations had not changed one iota—or, rather, as if it had not been separated into facts and figures.

Instantly a burly young man in a white coat appeared in front of him, pushing a little cart loaded with small multicolored bottles along the corridor, ringing a bell: "Lemonade, mineral water, fruit juice, Cola! . . ." The man from the mountain looked at him. He did not understand. He said:

"It's the water. Let me pass, son! I am late. People are thirsty."

Still later, when he found himself on his knees on the platform on top of his gurgling water bag, and while the last convoy passed by with the grinding sound of steel on steel, he still did not understand, any way he looked at it, what had happened in the space of a birth or a death: First he had faced a door he was unable to open, no matter how hard he tried. And then this train, disappearing at the horizon in a cloud of smoke, from which they had kicked him. He rose. Slowly. Found himself alone in this totally deserted station. Not a sound. Not a breath of air. He closed his eyes, opened them again. During that moment he had had a vision of his old rooster who had died at dawn, up there, in the village of Tselfat, his wings forever unfolded behind him, on a heap of charcoal.

He had been blind and not for one moment of his existence had he understood the world where he had wandered about in misery, suffering from ever-present hunger. And he, Raho, even though a Son of the Land, had never realized in his long existence full of patience and endurance, that endurance and patience were after all nothing but a fraud, an outrage to the soul, keeping humanity in misery and submission. But now he *knew*. He knew the value of the qualities one had cultivated and developed among the brothers of his race exactly. They were nothing but bits to cut the mouth: owners of the soil from time immemorial, the Berber peoples had done nothing but wait, wait and hope since the seventh century, wait and be extinguished—in the name of God and those who, to serve Him, had enslaved their brothers and now even denied them water. The shadows of the cave age were warmer, oh, yes! more humane than all the false lights of any religion.

His arms raised toward a sky ablaze with a million suns, he invoked the Almighty. Slowly, with great kindness, he told him:

"Allah, You have said in Your Book which saves the souls: *You, the Muslims, will be the intermediaries among people. Be witnesses before men, as the Prophet is a witness before you!* That is what You said. But Lord, are You a witness that now a Muslim may no longer be a Muslim and a human being less than human?"

He emptied his water bag over his head, down to the last drop. Why do ablutions or say prayers from now on? With the full weight of an old, very old patience, and with the voice of all the pasts of all generations which had preceded him, he cried:

"Aïn Taoujdate! Beddouza! Skoura-Aït Serhrouchen! . . . In him

23

and around him Islam was shattered; the Islam that had nourished him like no fire in this world and that had kept his pagan forces locked up in a prison. Pagan as at the beginning of time, his voice grew louder, grew as torrential as a stream of rocks of a mountain suddenly burst.

"Amizmiz! Bouskoura! Ida Ou Gnidif! Tilouggite-N'Aït-Isha! . . ."

And so it went: through the dry streets of the deserted city, along the tarred road and the steep path leading to Tselfat, he never stopped hurling the names of the rivers, the villages and the territories which in the course of the centuries and their faith his tribe had to leave, abandoning there the corpses of men and the corpses of their illusions.

"Tounfite! Tnine Chtouka! Tleta-D-Sidi Bouguedra, Zellija-Boubker, Ifrane, Zerhoun, Talsinnt, Tanannt, Oulad Sidi Mellahine, Oulmès, Oualidia, Dar Ould Zidouh, Al-Jadida, Azemmour!"

That same evening, he sold what there was to sell, paid his debt to the poor in order not to owe God or his religion—and went into the night toward the solitary mountain, he and his descendants to the last degree. Climbing to their last refuge, all felt they were descending into time, searching for their ancestors.

A World on the March

The respect for the ties of kinship adds to life
Mohammed

1

Through those who are sent, wave after wave to create the storm, through those who spread out and separate and call to arms, yes, that which is promised you will come! He will come when the stars will disappear, when the sky will break open, when the mountains will turn into dust, when the hour will be announced to the messengers. When will the day of reckoning come?

The day of reckoning had come and the face of the earth and its soul changed forever: hardly born, Islam had spread like lightning to the four horizons, surged like a tidal wave. And its sons, sons of the desert and the bare rock, carried it farther and farther into space and deeper into time, through the word and through the sword, through the hammering of their galloping horses' hoofs—convinced that the sun had risen on the very day of the Hegira and that each one of its rays had entered their chests, replacing the hearts of flesh and blood.

"My temple is the universe and my altar the heart of men!"

Moved by the divine word from the marrow of their bones to the range of their sharp eyes, racing towards the future standing upright in the stirrups of their horses, they had no homeland but Islam. They carried this homeland within them, in the East as in the West, on land as on the sea. Each rider, each horse was the messenger of God, carrier of the Message. The worldly empires those others had believed to be built on rock crumbled, all that was built on human foundations turned to dust. From the Indian Ocean to the Atlantic, not a simple board could float that was not Muslim.

With infinitely more distance from the conquerors or the conquered of three continents, a man who peacefully wandered the earth since the last quarter of the seventh century witnessed the coming and the event. A witness through all his senses, without a single word. In the name of Allah the all-merciful, the executioner had cut off his tongue—this same tongue that had lit and stoked the fire of the revolt in the very terms of the Koranic rites. Still warm, the executioner had dropped the tongue from the heights of a minaret at the hour of prayer. Around the mosque, immense flower beds honored God with the purples of the mallows, the bright red of the hibiscus, the fires of the beacons, the multicolored song of the calceolaria and the phlox. It was an evening in springtime.

Many sufferings and years later, the man without a voice slowly walked along the paved road leading to Cordoba. With patient, almost inconsistent steps he walked through this beginning of dawn in the Christian year of grace seven hundred and twelve—an old man, who seemed very frail but was full of life inside. What he could no longer express with the tongue of man, had clarified his thoughts during the long silence. The silence from words had in the end given him the most precious gift: the ability to be alone without being lonely. It had sharpened his eyes and ears, had rid his thoughts of dead tissue and had honed them to such an extent that, when a hand was held out to him, his thoughts sometimes went down right to the tips of his fingers. The soul of the pagan eras was alive in his blood, while he untiringly followed the path of life, walking on the heels of History. If the latter had begun with the new religion and was unfolding under his eyes, he could but admit its reality and its splendour. But he, Aït Yafelman, the Son of the Land, he dated back further than History, he dated back to what had preceded all human societies and what would probably one day survive them all: the animal kingdom. A centenarian roaming about the Islamic empire, he paid much closer attention to the roots of a civilization than to its top or its fruit. Like an oak or a redwood tree which had lived through centuries, he only trusted one master, lord of all that is born, lives and dies: Time.

Small, shriveled, as dry and knotty as a cudgel made of the wood of the Argan tree. Bald skull, milky-white sparse beard. Leather sandals with straps coming up to his knees. Wrapped in a length of unbleached wool without seams or sleeves, like the Moudarite Bedouins who thirty years earlier under the orders of the legendary emir Oqba ibn Nafi, had swept everything before them in one gigantic ride from Tripoli to the mouth of the Oum-er-Bia, on the Atlantic coast.

About a dozen arm spans behind the man, a camel with swollen udders, preceded by its shadow under the rising sun. Girted, with two gurgling water bags on its flanks, it carried the green banner of the Prophet between its humps and stowed on top of them, a five-stringed lute. Around its neck it carried a string of date pits, necklaces of amulets, tinkling bells made of silver, bronze and brass. Under the animal, a sand-colored camel colt, the size of a skinny donkey, wobbled on the unsteady legs it did not yet know how to use. Purple eyelids rimmed with long black lashes, its rosy snout always attached to a teat, its mother sometimes had to drag it along attached to her like this. Most of the time, she stopped to let the colt drink its fill. Then she gave a light roar like a signal that was final, swished her tail like a whip and rejoined the old man with a few leaps.

Azwaw never stopped walking. He did not even look back. He saw the shadow of the camel shorten in front of him—and all his wrinkles began to move, from his throat to the base of his nose and from his forehead to his lips, rippling like the alluvial deposits of a delta, giving birth to an open, happy smile. Life was still life! And it was all the more beautiful for just beginning, sharp, avid and triumphant. This little animal was no more than a week old. It had almost been still-born. Its mother had fallen into a ditch full of mud and rotting leaves, had rolled around in it, gasping for air, her mouth wide-open and dry, down there, before the Guadalquivir . . .

Azwaw had not hesitated for one moment. Whether animal or human, a female was a female, without any difference whatsoever when it came to procreation. Sometimes one had to help her, give her a human hand. He had plunged his arm into the uterus, up to his elbow, then up to his shoulder, then into the palpitating, burning womb, and there he had turned the colt who was in the wrong position, its head and limbs twisted. Slowly, his fingers spread out and half bent, very slowly, he had pulled it out by the head toward the light falling from the sky like a dazzling waterfall. He, the man from the Maghreb used to living under the sun, saw only a vague form moving softly through a liquid rainbow. As soon as he had touched it with his index, the water sack broke and the birth water mixed with the blood of life had inundated him from head to toe.

With quivering nostrils, like a primate of the Antiquity, he filled his lungs with the female humus odour, the scent of desire and of giving—the same pagan odor which suddenly surged from his far-away past, full of sensual pleasure and loam: the loam of his native river Oum-er-Bia where he had learned to swim like a halibut before he could walk. The sensual pleasure of the women with whom he had lain, filling them abundantly with his semen (his first wife who died one summer evening in the midst of orgasm, making a curious quacking sound, the second wife who enveloped everything with her golden fleece as if it were a blanket and whose belly he kneaded to get her ready for the act, but especially his daughter Yerma, who sex for sex resembled her mother. At any hour of the day or night, everywhere his member stood up or preceded him, on the patio under the open sky on a bed of cowhides exuding a beautiful bovine smell, in the fertile prairie on the side of the mountain where the dead were buried, up high in a smiling fig tree that always managed to put a ripe, juicy, plumb fig split open and red like a vulva, in front of his eyes at the moment of spasm. And always alive, never forgotten, coming back in a gallop, the fragrance of the village of Azemmour which the horsemen of the emir Oqba had destroyed down to the foundations on a luminous morning of the year 681.

On the village square, two men in the full vigor of manhood each held a shaft of the press and gave it a turn. The fragrance of the olive oil was then like the odor of the female, and the sea breeze carried it to the hills before the oil itself had run into the barrel, thick and black, sometimes touched with honey-colored flames when a ray of the morning star fell on it; under an open shed near the harbor the blacksmith's forge with its hammering and flying sparks, with its smell of burning charcoal and the dung that prolonged the life of the glowing coal; happily the millstone turns and turns under the paddlewheel and, from the low houses built of mud to the top of the highest trees, the whole surroundings smell of the barley dust that covers everything, including the eyelashes of passers-by. Cakes made of barley and onions sizzle gently on flat, red-hot stones. A group of nubile girls, chattering, laughing and ripe from the springtime within them, kneading balls of wet clay that smells of rut, shaping them into plates, pots, jugs. Within reach of their laughter, in front of the ovens where they spend the night to warm their bones during the summer as well as during the winter, the Ancients of the tribe plunge their arms up to the elbows into clay jars as tall as they, pull out strings of meat dripping with juice and spices, hang them on a cord strung between two flowering sycamore trees. From space to space, with a deafening noise, the flight of birds, sea gulls by the legions, wood pigeons, ibis, warblers, yellow-beaked ravens, flaming-red birds of paradise. On the banks of the river, among the gorse, gardens of pink flamingos, not one of them stirring. And slow, heavy like the blood in the veins of an old man, the lapping of the waters of the Oum-er-Bia above the village, then its roar at the mouth, where its boiling waters mingle with the waves of the ocean . . .

Happy and content, the camel breathed through her nostrils, licked her baby with wide swipes of her tongue, licked the hand of the man who had delivered her, and from her back to the tips of her ears, over her whole body, rippling waves came and went, like the rising tide —while from the East to the West of Andalusia, and up in the sierras, and down towards the Djebel Tariq, Gibraltar, and the African land, a whole world was being born. As far as the eyes and ears could reach, there were drums, flutes and *bendirs*; the biting voices of the saws, the sounds of the masses, of knocking, reverberated loudly from echo to echo.

"Clear me those banks," General Tariq Bnou Ziyyad had ordered. "I want to see the Oued-el-Kébir (the big river) from beginning to end and the enemy with my bare eyes, if there should be any left after my victory. This is were the capital of the empire will be built for all eternity. Cut down this forest and even the bushes. Tear out the grass. Dig up the soil and lift out the rocks and use them to built houses of God and palaces like none ever existed in this world. If there is a paradise, I want it now and right here, in this country of Al-Andalous where our paths have led us! I want the light of the seven skies to flow into my city of Cordoba and the life of every inhabitant, present or yet to be born, be gently rocked by water music—just as the music of God sings from the first to the last sura of the Book that moves the souls and made us move from the Arabic desert."

"Of water we have . . . "

Instantly, as if with one voice bursting forth from horizon to horizon, the army of Bedouins and Berbers took up the famous Koranic verse: *"Of water, we have created all living things."* The whinnying of the horses echoed from mountain to mountain.

Standing on the hill overlooking the Guadalquivir, General Tariq, short, slim, a cord of plaited hemp in the shape of a serpent around his forehead, had shouted with all his might:

"You are the people of tomorrow. From your toe nails to the roots of your hair, show your Islam to those you have conquered with your sword! If weapons are now silent in this province, their noise will be heard even louder some day in the future, of that I am sure. But I, Tariq Bnou Ziyyad, I want this day to come only at the end of our mission. And to accomplish this, we must not delay and finish this war by the only war there is: that of the spirit. God has been with us. He is still with us, but He will not always be with us. To deserve Him, we have to create His peace, His garden, His kingdom for centuries and centuries so that future generations, if ever they should become deaf and blind to the Spirit, will remember us and in their despair take us to witness, saying: 'where are our ancestors? They had built the golden age with their very souls.' Sons of the East and of the Berbers listen: the East is dying. It is behind you with its Damascus, its Bagdads and its endless divisions which inundate the earth with blood and falsify the word of God. Never will you go back there. You are here now, in the West, and it is as if you had just been born. Because I, I tell you, that from now on, it is here in the West that the sun of the world will rise! Just like the Prophet, each one of you has a liver: I want the best this liver is able to feel; and a brain: I want the best of what this brain is able to think; and a heart: I want the best of what this heart is able to love; and two hands: I expect them to work—Allah too! The past is over. You have only the future."

Blocks of sandstone or granite loosened with pickaxes, shovels or crowbars, torn from the soil by dozens of arms, pulled away with ropes ready to break past the walls of men with knees bent, hamstrings bulging, pulling and pitching from shoulder to shoulder, then cut on the spot into cubes, cylinders, arches, polished with bronze scrapers, smoothed like marble with buffalo skin glued to a block of wood, finally rolled on logs in the direction of the river, where they were hauled in by the boatmen, standing side by side, arms around each others' waists, sons of the Nile, the Tigris or the Oum-er-Bia. With stentorian voices, the *Qoussas*, the story tellers, went from group to group, spurring them on by singing about the exploits of one tribe and another, beating the drums and the *bendirs*, modulating the high-pitched desert flutes, celebrating the ancestors and their history, their endurance, their bravery, enlivening the spirit of the clan and, beyond the clan, the spirit of all the clans, instilled *esprit de corps*, while the strident voices of the women calling out could be heard intermittently. They huddled at the edge of the excavations that became deeper and deeper by the hour, picking up the shards and broken bits from the cut stones, grinding them in a mortar. Later the fine powder would be mixed with quicklime to make cement which would last forever. The most beautiful stones were brought in procession like offerings to the clearing. There, sitting cross-legged in front of his goatskin tent, an ancient sheik examined them one by one. He studied them for a long time, his look almost absent, examined their grain and texture before giving a signal to the porter standing in front of him like a statue.

The fingers of the old man began to move, slowly and methodically, sure of their art. With a sharp little sound, without ever stopping, the wooden hammer rose and fell; the chisel with a beveled point, held negligently between thumb and forefinger, went where it should, to the exact depth, engraved the first word which in days and seasons to come, would become a lively historical fresco, written with the words of God. The man blew calmly upon the letters and arabesques which formed under his eyes, dusted them with a falcon feather. Sometimes he smiled, talked to himself in a low voice: "This stone here will be the corner stone of the central arch of the mosque-cathedral . . . and this one, of oolite veined with onyx, will become *incha Allah* the main facade of a public fountain at the entrance to the market place. It was enough to put into relief what had gestated in nature for centuries and millenniums: prodigious designs that took your breath away. Down below, over the hill, artisans from Tangier and Azemmour and farther still, were already at work in their stalls, potters and ceramists from father to son. The indigo, the raw greens of life itself, were extracted from lichens only they knew of, the bright red they obtained by boiling a handful of cochineal in brine, and the ochres from the foothills of the Atlas and the blackish-brown of the soot obtained from calcified sheep bones, yes, the artisans would know how to let them burst into an explosion of color on this piece of sandstone here, in such a way that in days to come, the passer-by who would drink from the fountain, would first restore his soul, just by looking at this

o o o

Up above, in the forest of the hillside, the Berbers, Sons of the Land and of ancient times attacked the elm trees, the hornbeams, the holly oaks, the beeches, the larch trees. They had waged the war against the heavily-armed Visigoths in the trees, with slingshots and slip knots. Now that Cordoba was conquered, they were here, squatting on their heels in front of the forest, bare-chested, their forearms in an iron bracelet, as if they were meditating about History and its tortuous paths, an axe between their knees. And, only a moment later, they were flying through the branches, as light and agile as the maggots that jumped from branch to branch. Their faces turned up to the sky, their mouths open, the bards were dancing around in concentric circles, the three cords of their *guinmbri* resounding, chanting at the top of their voices praising the race and what bound it: the bonds of blood. The refrains were Koranic, or almost, testifying to the glory of the Lord of the universe, who, by His Word alone had given the *Imazighen*, the Berbers, vast territories and beautiful Spanish women to fertilize for the perpetuation of the species. And, baraka of barakas, the religion was OPEN TO ALL! It had taken into its folds all the conquered of previous days as equals and had turned them into craftsmen who helped shape the greatest victory of all, that of the entire community. It sufficed to adhere to the community like the bark to a tree, and after peace had returned, to seize a saw or an axe. From their base to the crown, notched at the roots, the trees fell. A long time later, the waves of combustion still reverberated beyond the four cardinal points. With the speed of a missile the bards jumped to the side, ran as fast as they could, chanting the tunes of long ago, when each Berber who reached adulthood planted a tree to witness his life. As for the woodsmen, they had already arrived at the foot of another giant of the forest, rubbing their hands as if they were washing them with soap. Thoughtful. Even stripped down to its innards, the land would always remain the land. One day the grass would grow again . . . and perhaps a different humanity.

Sitting astride on the felled tree trunks the men, whose craft—if not their life—was the love of wood, caressed the bark and the fresh wounds oozing sap. They touched the sap with the points of their forefingers, smelled it, tasted it, tongues clicking. The future burned them like no other fire in the world, shivering under their hands, already present and very intense. These elm trees here, lying full-length on the earth that had nourished them, how intoxicating the smell of their nard grass was, mingled with the smell of fresh earth! It affected the senses and the reason. The gnarls, as hard as granite, legions of cabinet makers, wood carvers and polishers would pass them on to one another in space and time. And out of them, they would create coffers, small boxes, spinning wheels, bellows, combs to be used by women to untangle their luxurious hair or to paint 'faux bois', low, round tables which the fingers of goldsmiths would set with precious stones and mother-of-pearl for the pleasure of a shared meal. The copper beeches, smooth and resistant, were expected by a tribe that had come from Tinges, Tangier, waiting within earshot, settled on the river banks with women and children and a forest of tents. For everyone of them it was a matter of family honor: they were carpenters from father to son and from mother to daughter. Beams. Corner posts. Braces and cross-pieces. Lintels, door frames. Not a single nail, not one iota of metal, but knots of beeches carved into tenons and pegs. Glue made of fish bones to make them glide into the mortise and hold them there forever . . . And this oak tree here (may God rest its noble soul in His paradise!) would be sawed lengthwise, the thickness of a man's arm, such as it was, still green. Dried in the shade and then in the moon light to preserve its variegated patterns, reddish brown, it would be treated with an abundance of linseed oil, and finally it would be preserved with the smoke of resin sizzling on the coals with myrrh and benzoin. In one year or in five, that is to say, tomorrow, it will open up before the stranger having come to visit the city. It will open up slowly, majestically, having been crafted into a double door leading to the gardens of a palace, being itself a perfumed garden in every season and where each flower carved patiently and lovingly depicts a letter of the "Fatiha," the first suras of the Koran, the one of the Opening.

2

The rumbling of breaking rocks, trees falling down like thunder out of the skies, the voices of tools and the sounds of people amplified like a waterfall, reverberating endlessly, happy rhythms of the multitudes, chants, dances and music—this birth of a universe in which all races and peoples worked together, Azwaw Aït Yafelman felt this birth young and ardent in his very old body, while slowly, setting one foot in front of the other, he walked along the road to Cordoba, followed by the camel and her colt. When he reached the edge of the forest, everything was silent. All of a sudden. There rose the midday prayer.

Allahou akbarou Allahou akbar!
There is no God but God
and Mohammed is His prophet

The woodsman who acted as muezzin was some twenty measures above the ground, holding on to the crown of a lotus tree. He had put the sharp edge of his axe into the tree trunk, and standing upright, he shouted the message to the four corners of the earth, to the living and beyond. He was a man who did not stand out from the crowd, his features ordinary, black-haired and swarthy. But there was his voice. Immense and full of pathos, the voice changed, rising from the deep sounds to the extreme high notes of the desert flutes, changed its register, became tragic, then a burst of hope, fell like a lark in flight, light and peaceful like a breath. Men, women and children stood motionless, one with his rock, the other with his pick axe or his hammer. At the very moment when the muezzin opened his lips, they did nothing but listen, made not a single move.

Come to prayer!
Come to salvation! . . .

Azwaw had not slowed down one iota. Suddenly he heard no one, nothing—except his own voice. His voice, with the richness of bronze had resounded from the heights of the minarets of Damascus, of Mecca, of Medina, Cairo, Tangier, Alexandria, rung from the mountains, at the foot of the springs as on the estuary of the rivers, everywhere in the Empire. His voice alone had touched the myriad souls like lightning, more than any book. Azwaw took the words of the Koran and those of the rite into his mouth, made them go down into his intestines and then brought them back cleaned of their human tissue, liberated of their intellectual meaning that privileged the brain alone to the detriment of the enormous rest: the faculty to create words, to hear them, to touch them, to feel them and react to them as if they were human beings. Their emotional charge would be overwhelming. And this is how it was: by the inflections of the voice alone, behind each word surged forth from time immemorial the remembrance of OUM-AL-KITAB, the "Mother of the Book." Intensely irrational, this *source of the word in its virgin state* engulfed the consciousness of the people like a ground wave risen from the dawn of the ages. With a painful and at the same time serene yearning, it brought back the memory this other life which had belonged to the children of Adam and Eve before the beginning of the world, and to which humanity, suffering and erring in this world, by the grace of God, king of men, father of men, would return in the end, all of them, without exception, the conquerors and the conquered, evolved or in the state of larva, Jews, Muslims, Nazarenes or idol worshippers . . . When he came down from the minarets or from the mountains, Azwaw Aït Yafelman had difficulties to clear a path for himself among the mighty of the day. Generals, cadis, emirs were in the first row of the crowd, prostrate, their foreheads on the ground and sobbing. People fought to kiss his hands, touch the hem of his coat. They opened their homes and hearts to him, were honored by the trace of his footprints.

"Speak to us, sheik, speak so that we may understand Islam."

Though he was a conqueror, one among them had said to him, suddenly humble and small before his glory:

"Sheik, oh sheik of Islam, explain this riddle to me: how is it that your words are mightier than all our swords put together?"

"I don't know, Emir. Perhaps because I don't have a sword."

"Ha!" the emir had said. "May God forgive me."

He had pulled his sword out of its sheath, had broken it under his heel, his eyes red from crying. Repeating:

"May God forgive me!. God forgive the conquerors we believed ourselves to be! He alone has the power."

o o o

And now, across time and space, an old man walked along a path known only to himself, across Islam and the devastated forest. If he moved his lips and the stub of his tongue, he was not aware of it. The sounds he uttered were perhaps half-way between a complaint and a cry. But he, son of the pagan soil, he heard them with perfect clarity like so many chants of triumph rising from the depth of his being— the true language of the Berbers of Ancient Times who had done very well without any sort of religion. Paradise was down here, hell in heaven! Whoever they might be, Azwaw Aït Yafelman knew that the Gods living in heaven were the worst enemies of the human race, for not one of them was a human being. And their reign had been and would never be anything but a mutilation of life, witness the servant of Allah, the All Merciful, who had mutilated him in the flesh and in his faith . . . this Islamic faith which in spite of everything had burned him like no fire on earth. By cutting off his tongue and his words, his torturer had freed him at the same time of his illusions about the new religion. And that was all for the best! Yes, all for the best, because it had made him return to his very distant origins, to the time where there had been neither dreams nor words—nothing but life and death. This is what he talked to himself about with inarticulate sounds he alone could understand, while he went towards his destiny, his soul calm and patient.

The crowd did not know who he was, nor where he came from, not even what it was doing. All they had seen was the sacrilege and that had been enough for them: a tramp who ambled quietly in the midst of the motionless believers who listened to the call for prayer. Already the crowd was surging towards him, with thousand hands, thousands of screaming voices. And at that moment it happened: a giant oak tree, half notched at its base, suddenly cracked with a long tearing sound and started to fall directly on the old man.

Two events dumbfounded the crowd. Between the two of them, the charge of the believers stopped abruptly; the clamors had culminated in a paroxysm of fear, then died as if a sudden paralysis had struck these thousands of men. Azwaw had neither hurried nor slowed down his steps. He had not turned on his heels, nor had he jumped to one side. He had simply lifted his arm above his head—and this had been the first event: the tree at once changed its direction and fell a little farther, a stone's throw away. Exactly at the spot where the old man would have stood had he tried to flee to avoid the falling tree.

The oak tree rebounded several times as it thrashed on the earth, the mother that had nursed it. Sounds of its death struggle followed by reverberations and echoes as far as the ear could reach. And a long time later, silence. A rain of silence. Nothing but the panting breath of the men and the far-away sound of a bird, a night hawk. Shy at first, becoming braver as time went on, people started to murmur here and there, exchanged comments in snatches of conversation overlapping one another. The old man had the baraka. That was certain. Of no particular age, dressed as he was here in his piece of un-bleached wool, he must at least be one of the companions of the Prophet—may the grace and divine peace be with him!

"And I, I tell you that he knows the future."

"You are blaspheming. Only the Creator knows the future."

"Perhaps. But *he too*. He knew that this tree could not touch him, that his hour had not come."

"Have you heard about these strange creatures versed in the science they call *dhamyadhi*? Some of them can just look at you and you become transparent, your insides, bones, marrow and all the thoughts you even hide from yourself. Transparent like spring water. They penetrate the future with their 'divining tables'. It is a good thing to stay far away from them."

"By Allah, the All Powerful, the camel was not frightened either, nor was her young. Just as if they put themselves in their master's care. How do you explain that thistle of logic, doctor of law, you who know the Koran and the hadiths by heart?"

"There is an explanation and there isn't. God has said: 'we have created heaven and earth and all things between them'. Besides, all this is a dream."

"God bless you, wise man! It's a pleasure of paradise to hold one's ear close to your mouth. But explain a little more to the ignorant that I am. Open the words."

"In the darkest night, you will always see what your secret desires expect to see. And in the hardest heart, you will always find what is most tender: the blood that nourishes it. It is the same with the testimony of our senses. We see the skin of our fellow men and that is enough for us to judge them by. We don't know how to listen to the blood that courses in them."

"Nothing. I understand nothing of your words. They don't arrive at my head. Add a few simple and smooth words to your constipated ones."

"Oh sons of Adam!" a stone cutter cried out, swinging his mallet. "Oh you who believe in the Book descending from heaven in clear and intelligible Arabic, I ask you truly: what is the meaning of your covering up reason like you are doing now and buying superstitions for the price of enlightenment? I assure you that I saw, saw with my own Bedouin eyes, a liana thick like this hold back the tree mid-way in its fall. It is this liana and not magic, that made the tree fall over there, behind the hillock. In Islam, there are no mysteries and no miracles!"

"May God prolong your life, brother. Don't get angry. I am a Bedouin like you and a Muslim as well. And it is my belief that my eyes are as sharp as yours, look for look. I have seen this: *he saw nothing*. He did not even deign to lift his head towards the tree that was falling toward him from its full height. So, my dear countryman, how do you explain this small detail in the Arabic of clear reasoning?"

A woman came slowly forward. Her arms were loaded with firewood. In a toneless voice she said:

"Al-Khadir."

With the speed of the wind, the word flew from mouth to ear, from the summit of the hill to the banks of the Guadalquivir. It was as if all at once, all tongues had been wrung dry until the last drop of the last word of the tribe. And all began to shiver, looking at this apparition risen from obscurity, who stepped over stones and tree stumps, continuing on his way as if nothing had happened . . . Al-Khadir! Each time he had manifested himself on earth, it had been the beginning of a new era. He had met Moses where the two seas flow together and advised him on his mission: the infinite and continuous reality of the universe in which the reality of mankind, with all its knowledge, all its intelligence and all its power, was infinitely small, drifting like a straw in the wind. A prophetic mission only made sense if it abandoned all human logic and obeyed only the flux of world order . . .

Men, women and children stood transfixed, they only looked, held their breath. And none of them could evoke the supreme name (Al-Khadir, to whom God had granted eternal life) without being seized by vertigo that twisted their senses, broke the chain of ideas and of memory, shaking time and space, breaking down the doors of the past and the future: one day, the beginning and the end of every living being would meet, the alpha would become omega and there would be no more death. And here he was among them, on this Andalusian soil, at the beginning of the eight century . . .

That is when the second frightening event occurred. It was a bard who provoked it, the most ancient of the Ancients of the Berber tribe. He had broken away from the crowd and joined the man with the camel. Step for step, he walked alongside of him. Scrutinized him intensely, his chest leaning forward, his head turned three-quarters. He carried a drum on a shoulder strap: the barrel of its oblong shape was made of buffalo hide, as hard as ebony, so hard that it was used to make shields that withstood any arrow; the bottom was covered with goatskin, attached with cat gut; the strap was braided of women's hair—all that was left of his two dead wives, except for two dozen children, who in turn had procreated and sired legions of vigorous sons and daughters. It was one of those drums from the Atlas that a generation of men had been beating and the sound of which resembled mountain thunder so closely, that it was often mistaken for the latter. Slowly, very gently, the bard turned the drum to rest on his stomach and touched it with his finger tips. Deep as a well, the voice of the drum rose to reverberate among hill tops. Another drum answered, coming from the walls of the city; then others still, between the sky and the earth. Without stopping, their resonance wove across space, binding the present to the past and it was like the intoxicating voice of the native river finally found again, the Mother of Spring with its fertile, mute, heavy waves irrigating abundantly the plains and the sons of liberty. Its sons.

Master! . . . Master! . . . Master! . . .

In pairs, the Berbers came flying down the from trees, jumped to the ground feet together, throwing away their axes, arms outstretched, and trance-like pushed towards the ancestor of the tribe, towards their legendary master who long ago had forged the souls of his people with courage, endurance and the whip.

Master! . . . Master! . . . Master! . . .

Not dead! He had not died! Their faces beamed, their eyes shone and it was as if the spring of the whole world were born again in them and around them. In groups, whole families together, the Berbers came from everywhere, clapping their hands, singing, dancing. The loud yells of the children who ran among the legs of their elders, the strident "You-yous" of the women, who untied their hair and let it fly around them like living ribbons, letting it dance from left to right and from right to left, resounded while the beating of the drums came closer, was amplified, filling the air around them. They quickly gathered dry wood, tied it into bundles with young willow shoots, dipped them into a barrel of tar and fastened them to long, green sticks. One by one, the torches lit up in the bright sun. Smoking, sputtering, they formed a gigantic cluster where the Ancestor and the bard faced each other, smiling. And then, they slowly made the sign of ancient times over their heads: a fish surrounded by a star.

Master! . . . Master! . . . Master! . . .

The *bendirs* and desert flutes added their voices to the drums, quickening the rhythm to make the blood boil in their veins. All the instruments resounded with the same liveliness, tirelessly repeating the same notes, three short followed by three long: the oath of OUM-ER-BIA . . . THE-OATH-OF-OUM-ER-BIA . . . Hundreds of feet stomped in the same rhythm like hoofs of trampling horses. The ground shook, the dust rose in clouds as high as the people. Those who were not Berbers huddled in small, frightened groups, trying to see, if not understand what was happening in the forest. But the Berbers pushed them back without consideration: perhaps these people out-numbered them, but then they were only Arabs and other Levantines—in other words, newcomers to History. Conquerors and bearers of civilization in the name of God they might be, but that did not make them part of the immemorial blood community, the *Imazighen*.

o o o

The chief of the work site, Emir Badruddin ibn Zoubaïr, camped in a tent village under the ramparts of the city, in the midst of his clan and his Praetorian guard. Slender and supple, sporting a beard, he was dressed in a fine green and gold silk tunic from the Yemen. He sat cross-legged in a circle of books. When he was finished with one, he put it back in place and opened another one, sighing: *"Bismallah! In the name of the Lord!"* He had sworn not to leave his circle unless absolutely necessary. Around him, as far as the eyes and ears could reach, the Andalusian Islam was being built, stone by stone, an undertaking of man. He, Emir Badruddin, wanted to embrace the entire science of men. This was his only earthly subsistence, day and night, even in his dreams—except for the camel's milk which had been his only food and drink since he was very young.

"Unless you know what has happened before you were born, you will always remain a child . . . " Drawn in Aramaic calligraphy, the treatise he held on his knees was overwhelming. To penetrate it, one needed total concentration, the same profound meditation in which its author had conceived it towards the end of his life. He was dead and buried long before Islam had arrived. But his spirit remained. More fertile than ever. Was it possible that a man who had lived three or four centuries before the Revelation, during the era of the shadows, had explained with such clarity what he could not know? These en-lightening words over which the Koranic scholars racked their brains, bit their teeth out? But . . . but in that case he was a Muslim before the word? Or perhaps religion was but a reflection, a drop of the river Truth?

Like lighthouses in the long night of humanity, such human beings connected earth and heaven, and the oldest Antiquity to this eight century. Islam had an obligation to revive their memory, to take them to its bosom to open up to the world. To become an adult by knowing the past.

The emir Badruddin pressed his temples with both hand, once again read the old manuscript written on the skin of a tiny sheep. Let us see! It was not so long ago that the Arabs were blind in their obscurantism, without other laws or beliefs than those of their desert. And now, hardly eighty years after the death of the Prophet, they had spread all over the earth, from the Euphrates to the Ganges and from the Nile to the Guadalquivir, masters of defunct peoples and civilizations. They were proud of their emirs of Europe, of Africa and of Asia, and of their emirs of the sea. But he, Badruddin ibn Zoubaïr, considered himself an emir of the spirit only. He was born at Dimash-Shamm, had studied his first book in the Khorassan, devoured volume after volume in the libraries of Askandariya, in the land of Misr. He belonged to the followers of the Omeyyads, he had been with them from stage to stage, throughout History, as far as Cordoba. To reward him for his faithfulness, they had offered him a province. He had told them softly:

"The most sumptuous houses will fall into ruin. And the most beautiful orchards, who knows if they will not be barren one day? Give me something that will last: books."

How many years had he left to live? *Mektoub*, all was written. He knew it and gave thanks to the Sublime Creator for each day which miraculously was added to his life, like unexpected fruit late in the season. Perhaps his destiny would allow him to fulfill his tasks as an exemplary Muslim, to be a mediator of East and West, North and South, to learn other languages besides those of the Koran, to listen with his heart to the greatest number possible of voices who had fallen into silence—and to transmit anew their sense to the community of Islam. A birth was finally nothing but a small death if it happened under a bell-jar. A birth concerned not only the mother giving life to her child, nor to the father, nor to the relatives, closely related or not. A birth only acquires its full meaning in space and time if all of humanity participates in it.

The emir Badruddin was slowly turning the mouldy pages of the old manuscript. He had stuck his little finger into his ear to listen only to peace—the peace of the author who had filled these pages with the future. But the higher the sun rose, the louder the noise grew down there in the forest. It disturbed his meditation, closed in on him in almost palpable waves.

"Praise be to God!" he murmured, closing the book. He prostrated himself, said a short prayer. Then he sent for a guard. Very gently he told him:

"Brother, go and bring some of my silence to our brothers. Go and God bless you."

The guard left on horse back, preceded by two strong, well-built heralds (one of them exerted himself blowing a horn while the other shouted orders his own ears could not hear in the hellish uproar, something like: "Make way! Make way for the guardsman, the envoy of his excellency, Emir Badruddin ibn Zoubaïr, may God keep him!" The guardsman came back a few minutes later, alone and on foot. His clothes in shreds, his face bruised, he said without waiting:

"Islam has left them, Lord Emir! In my opinion it has never been but a thin coat of varnish for them. There they are, Berbers and barbarians like before. At this hour, they are nothing but *majnoun*, possessed from head to toe, savage and diabolic. They are in a black rebellion, my eyes and ears have witnessed it, Lord Emir. In your place, with all due respect, I would get in touch with His Honor, the Governor. Or better yet, I would go and fetch General Tariq. He and his army are camped only half a day's march from here. He would know how to subdue them. He is the chief of us all."

Spitting out a tooth, he added:

"There is an *afrith*, a devil, among them, surged from obscurity, a hellish Satan not taller than this, of no particular age, moth-eaten and mangy like this old sheep skin you are sitting on. They are about to offer a mass of fire to him. They are slashing their wrists, fighting to be first to spill some blood at his feet. They call him 'the Master' . . . 'the Master of the Hand' . . . "

These last words had hardly been spoken when the emir Badruddin knew immediately that something fatalistic had happened, something of great consequence. Shivering all over, he rose.

He rose, stepped over the books and without so much as a glance at the guardsman, who stared at him open-mouthed, he took off his tunic, dressed in a mended old smock full of holes. All the while he was reciting the sura "YA-SIN," the heart of the Koran. His voice was choked with emotion. For at present he knew that the world had come full circle: the man from the past had arrived at last. His legend was alive in the four corners of the Empire. It had many versions. Some people claimed that he could give life by laying-on of hands. That is why he was called the "Master of the Hand." Others swore by the salute of their souls that he could make the desert flower. The governor himself, Qaïs Abou Imran, offered all the riches of Cordoba to those who would bring the old man to him, for he was skilled in midwifery and could help in desperate cases. The governor's wife had come to the end of her pregnancy, burning with fever and almost paralyzed by some unknown disease. All the doctors of Andalusia, even the Jewish scholars with all their knowledge and History, had failed with their potions, their sitzbaths and their blood letting. Qaïs adored his wife. He called her *Kawkeb-al-Gharb*, "Star of the West." And on the child she carried in her womb, on whether it would live or die, depended the destiny of his house. Qaïs Abou Imran was a Sherif, a descendant of the Prophet.

The emir Badruddin left his tent, started to walk towards the forest on his bare feet. Another destiny, much larger, was in jeopardy: Islam. For having used his eyes in the thorough study of the old wizards' books, he knew for a fact that the four seasons of life inexorably ruled the lives of the peoples. Some of them had known only the springtime of their lives. Others had matured, given abundantly of their fruit in the summer. Then autumn had come and their slow decline.

The winter of time had effaced the work of their hands and their foot prints. And it was as if they had never existed at all. Full of youthful vigor, the Arabs had taken over from the people fallen from their ancient glory. They were but at the beginning of their triumphant spring. They were persuaded that their reign had no other limit than eternity . . . precisely because they possessed a force greater than themselves: the Message.

While he went on his way to meet the Master of the Hand, the emir Badruddin, divested of all signs of nobility and wearing only his Berber garment, felt alternately waves of heat and pin pricks of cold. An Arab himself, he never worried about his fellow-men or their descendants of the generations yet to come. In four, ten or fifteen centuries, the last emir on earth—if indeed any were left—might well be a ruminant. He, Badruddin ibn Zoubaïr could not help that. What was more important to him than his bones and marrow, was the Message, the soul of his soul. He ignored nothing, not even a shadow, of this very old man at whose feet he would soon prostrate himself. Neither his name, Azwaw, nor that his tongue had been cut, nor the long, enduring battle he had fought for the perpetuation of his race, time being his only weapon. Perhaps time would see the descendants of the sherifs and the emirs become sedentary and crumble under their own power, and only with a vague feeling of nostalgia remember the Message, which had inspired the Bedouins of long ago—and time would see the Berber peoples who had patiently waited in obscurity, standing straight, ready to take the torch away from Islam, survive them.

"*We have made the Book come down during the night of Destiny . . .* " Emir Badruddin chanted in a low voice. He seized the torch a happy-looking young woman held out to him and joined the circle of the singers and dancers.

"*And who will ever tell you what the night of Destiny is?*"

He believed he knew. It was so simple, really: it sufficed that just one believer stood at the cross-roads, in the right place, at the right moment.

49

3

General Tariq Bnou Ziyyad had burned his vessels. Standing at the edge of the rock that was to carry his name all through History, he declared his faith in two granitic sentences:

"Sons of Adam and of Islam, the enemy is ahead of you and behind you, the sea. All you have to do is to conquer or die." Close to him, a man from the East, in the full vigor of manhood, looked at the roaring waves, his head bent. Without even turning around, without even looking at him, Tariq kicked him in the back and into the sea. He said:

"Here we have one already who chose to return to the old past. Who wants to follow him?"

Across from him, forming a moon crescent, three thousand warriors from the Atlas showed their teeth right to their gums: it was their way of expressing the pride they felt in their commander. Three thousand toughs from the tribes of Zaer, Bani Snassen and Aït Yafelman who had forced a terrible life on the Arab conquerors for thirty years. Behind him, the ships drifting the whole breadth of the strait, were aflame. And with the ships burned the food that a few erring souls had loaded thinking of their stomach in days to come. At his feet, the general had half-a-dozen bags of onions. He took one, held it over his head so that all might see. He said:

"Labsal, good red onions from home. You will each get one at the end of the day to season the meat you will have killed along the road."

The storm of laughter that suddenly shook the Sons of the Land made every living creature for miles around, flee. It happened on a fine morning in the year seven hundred eleven.

o o o

Six months earlier, a night so stormy the sky seemed to explode. A commando of five men, independent from one another where decisions and execution of their tasks were concerned. Yet united like the five fingers of one hand. Totally naked, except for a cord rolled around their waists. Their heads shaved, their bodies coated with a mixture of oil and sooth. Their names were Aghrou, Hawch, Hampsal, Zid, Biloud. Between the five of them, they did not even have one century of existence.

A felluca sailing from Tangier had landed them on the Iberian coast which they saw for the first time. A flash of lightning showed them a low house a stone's throw from the beach. They approached it and sneaked around it like snakes. It was a peasant's house, built of wood and mud, low with thickset walls, with a door one could only pass by bending in two and a small, narrow window on the side. And farther on, beyond the fence, a stable built of tree trunks and branches.

Zid and Biloud swung themselves on the thatched roof. Zid unrolled one or two lengths of his rope. At the end of the rope there was a slip knot, ready for use. He crouched just above the door and waited. Biloud was sitting at the square opening that served as chimney. He too was waiting. Aghrou took up position in front of the window. His facial features were so mobile, he could take on any look he chose. He took on the mask of a terrifying demon and did not move a muscle. During that time, Hawch and Hampsal had moved over to the stable. They lifted the latch on the door and entered like two wolves, more silent than silence itself. Their nostrils quivered at the warm smell of the chickens. And they felt happy when they heard the snuffles of a pig and the snoring of a Nazarene. They knew what they had to do. It was as easy as poking a finger into a piece of butter.

The man who had been sleeping soundly now was asleep for good. He would never snore again, his adams apple broken by a quick chop of the hand. And this same hand that had just killed garotted the pig and pulled it out of the stable at the end of the rope, screaming like the damned impure it was.

At the same time, Hawch, his legs stretched out in front of him like hatchets, caught the chickens and plucked them alive, one by one, tearing out fistfuls of feathers. Then he threw them out into the night, naked and screaming.

Waking up suddenly, the farmer tore off the door of his house more than he opened it. Thunder was rolling and lightning split the sky in blinding rays. His eyes popping, he saw his chickens scattering in all directions, saw his pig rolling on its back. He heard them agonize in their torment. He tried to understand. He reached behind him, looking for a pitch fork. And without any warning, he jumped into the air: standing firmly on his legs, Zid had hung him short and high. When the corpse had ceased to jerk, Zid waited for the space of an orgasm before he let him drop. Then Biloud went into action. He stuck his head into the chimney hole and started to make a series of uninterrupted animal noises. He imitated to perfection the meowing of a wild cat, the metallic laughter of a starving hyena, a roaring lion. And fell silent.

Down below, someone had managed to light an oil lamp. The hand holding the lamp quivered like the heart of a bird, making the flames and smoke dance. Deathly pale, haggard, the shadows preceded by their sobs and lamentations did what fear commanded them to do: they ran. They ran to the door, but turned back towards the window when they saw the corpse on the threshold, saw the devil looking in through the window, screamed with terror as they looked up the chimney where another black-faced monster was jubilant, lips drawn back. Placidly, Biloud watched the culmination of fear. When he felt it had reached its limit, he jumped down. With him entered the other members of the commando. They broke everything in the house before attacking its inhabitants. The woman had thrown herself at their feet, imploringly. They pulled her up by the hair, spread her legs, raped her and brutalized her, beating her like putty. Kicked her. But they did not kill her. They beat the children too, three or four of them, without restraint or pity. Among them was a little girl with the face of an angel, who in spite of the beatings had not shed a single tear nor made any sound. Perhaps she did not feel the pain or was feeble-minded. Hawch took care of her. He took her by the neck and with his teeth, tore her ear off. He chewed it, spit it out. His mouth full of blood, he said:

"The Moors, that's us. We are the Moors."

And all of them repeated as if with one voice:

"We are the Moors. We will come back."

They disappeared into the shadows that had vomited them, among the rolling thunder and the heavy rains falling from the sky. That same night, other commandos, in other parts of the coast of the land of the Visigoths, spread death and desolation. Before leaving, they all proffered the same menace:

"We are the Moors. We shall come back."

And they returned, more merciless than ever.

o o o

Overlooking the harbor and the city of Tinges like a guard post, a small, lonely house built on the hill side. General Tariq Bnou Ziyyad sat on his open patio, his legs stretched out under a low round table. He had his breakfast accompanied by a concert of birds greeting the rising sun. He chewed his barley cake slowly, carefully, without moving his jaws, as if he had all the time in the world. After each bite, he took a swallow of whey followed by a purple olive. One by one he collected the stones on the table as the chiefs of the commandos knelt before him and gave him their reports. With sleepy eyes, General Tariq listened to them in silence, his face betrayed nothing, seemed as asleep as his eyes. Delicately he dropped an olive stone on the table to signal approval or the end of the interview. When the talking had ceased and he was left alone with the music of the birds, he gathered the little pile of olive stones, counted them and recounted them and divided them into a configuration as jumbled up as the underground ramifications that ruled the tribes of the Maghreb since the beginning of time.

Military strategy was one thing, he knew that. But it was not only this one thing, abstract and fleeting, without any real hold on the soldiers. They could not see farther than their own lives. Since he was very young, Tariq had studied the behavior of animals in combat. The bravery of the lion was certain, direct and very noble; but it lasted only the time of the stalking and of the attack. After that . . . after that, the king of the animals lay down and snored, its belly filled. As for the wolves, they attacked in gangs, by ruse and continued baiting. Even after they had eaten their fill, they slept with one eye open, remaining vicious and mangy warriors. At present, Tariq Bnou Ziyyad had total power. As a commander of the Islamic army, what was important to him to the highest degree was not so much the triumph of Islam, but that of the men, his men, whom he prepared to send into battle. If they were victorious, they would believe all the more. They would be younger, more ardent, more generous believers than they had ever been. Then one could ask anything of them. They would believe that it was their accomplishment, if not that of God. And perhaps they would accomplish miracles in building the new society that was Tariq's supreme goal.

Twenty-seven olive pits. He put twenty-six of them into the pockets of his goatskin tunic. The last one he weighed in the hollow of his hand . . . Twenty-six tribes united by the immemorial ties of blood, yet hereditary enemies among each other. Before he could fight a war as such (and the enemy would certainly not put up battalions of weaklings and yellow-livered men), he had to extract from each tribe the marrow of its aggressiveness, the essence of what made up a warrior worthy of that name. By sending them in small commandos for what he called the "appetizers" of the conquest of Spain, he was sure in advance that each clan would make it a point of honor to outshine the other in determination and cruelty. In this way, their aggressiveness would be turned away from the principal enemy (the Arabs who had conquered the Berbers and imposed their own laws on them) and would entirely and more murderously be directed at another enemy: the infidel.

No. Wars could not be waged with prayers and beads. He, general of Islam, had assigned himself a gigantic task that went beyond war and peace, to save what was left of the original Oumma and, if necessary, create a new community and irrigate it with new blood—elsewhere than in Arabia, in the East or in the Maghreb. The world had known a golden age that had lasted thirty-six years, first under the rule of the Prophet, then under the rule of the first four "well-guided" caliphs: Omar, Abou Bakr, Othman and Ali. At that time, peace and justice reigned supreme, for the common interest came first. There was not even a state. Only consensus. Each heart had become a garden . . . Then came Mou'awiyya, the founder of the Omeyyads, and especially his son, Yazid. Then the interests of his family and his dynasty triumphed in a blood bath. It happened in Karbala, in the year six-hundred-and-eighty, at the same time the legendary Oqba ibn Nafi carried the green banner of the Prophet right to the borders of the Atlantic Ocean. Since then, the Muslims all over the world, Blacks, Whites, Yellows, had begun to distrust their princes who had taken the power by the law of their arms, and they considered them a last resort, who had completely forsaken their religion. If the believers dreamed, it was only of the past, their refuge in great sadness.

Tariq was not the slightest bit nostalgic. But he still had his thirty-six teeth and the skin of his teeth. Oh yes, he would recreate his own Hegira—his total escape—in the company of real Berbers, strong and down-to-earth, who knew only their commander and a certain Master of the Universe of whom they spoke in terms as concrete as a rock, as warm as the sun. Yes, he would rebuild the golden age. Neither tomorrow nor later, as the Scriptures of the Nazarenes said, but in this world, here and now and with vigor. To accomplish this, he would not hesitate to provoke fate rather than suffer it—this old destiny which could mean life as well as death, and which was, after all, nothing but a combination of doubt and temporization. And to hell with the devout stewing in their contrition, fatalistic and puny like their testicles! If they meditated, it was about their own shadow, hoping for salvation in the Great Beyond . . . and, if appropriate, let Allah rain some ideas and resolve the human problems from beginning to end. It would be just as well to abandon those grumblers on the edge of the road, without any more delay, like so much garbage. The caravan of Islam would only be better off if it increased its pace. Time was not cattle, but rather the thorny stick behind the cattle. Coldly, without a shadow of a doubt, Tariq Bnou Ziyyad was already sure in his blind belief, that the model Muslims of tomorrow would be the conquered of tomorrow, the Iberians, indeed the Franks.

He took the left-over olive pit between his thumb and forefinger, contemplated it for a long time as if he tried to guess at fate, the ultimate question of the future. Then, with a flick of the finger, he threw it in the air, caught it with his open mouth and cracked it with his teeth. His brow wrinkled, his nostrils quivering with pleasure while the juice ran along his tongue, bitter and, my God, so delicious. It was so simple. It sufficed to break the carapace of men to make them worthy of the Message which was now entrusted to them—or to dig anywhere, among the rocks or in the driest desert, to find water. Water was the source of life. It was everywhere. Everywhere. One had to take the trouble to look for it, go down and look for it in the belly of the earth. Light was not at the surface, but on the inside, deep within the sons of Adam. And if Islam was a gift of the Lord of the universe to the human race, it was also and especially a goal to strive for, to deserve, to be conquered with the force of their fists and the sweat of their souls. Tariq considered faith that went only skin-deep like a simple coat of paint that would fade as time went by. The *faith* of the *faith*, the core of life, Tariq was ready to extract it from within the people, ferociously determined to succeed where the Muslims of the East had failed and divided the Oumma into a multitude of sects, pursuing each other from Mecca to Al-Askandariaya and from Damascus to Baghdad, killing one another with daring and hate, all in the name of God and sincerely believing. And yet, the Koran states clearly: *"To kill a single human being is to kill the entire human race."* With all his life's strength, General Tariq Bnou Ziyyad had decided to conquer Spain to the limits of its borders and the end of the centuries, to establish there a young vigorous Islam, knowing neither decline nor death. Ever. Ever . . .

A young captive, exhausted to the point of dragging herself rather than walking, entered the patio. With his eyes, Tariq caressed her curves, from her ankles to the tip of her breasts, while she painfully placed one foot in front of the other. Not for one moment did he raise his eyes to her face, that was for later when the fire would consume him. When she approached the table in order to clear it, he snapped his fingers and, timidly, she sat down next to him, moving softly, her vulva suddenly swollen. He did not say a word, only slid his hand between her thighs, just under her pubic hair, where the best parts of a woman lay. His hand did not move at all, did not caress. Only its presence and its warmth.

They remained like that, side by side, listening to the concert of the birds, she quivering, he absolutely immobile. When he felt she was tender like a good dish of *hargma*, a lamb stew which had simmered a long, long time, he inhaled her spicy, female odor with both nostrils. It drove him mad and he possessed her. On the table. Then when the table noisily broke into pieces, he continued on the tiles without pausing to take a breath. At the moment when the second orgasm (the most complete, the most powerful of all) shook her, he looked at her. He scrutinized her. And, as always, he was overcome with astonishment: how in the name of God could a face, so ill-favored by nature, full of pimples, twisted and as grey as a dish rag be transfigured to such an extent—become beautiful, beautiful through joy?

"*Allah akbar!*" he shouted at the top of his lungs. "I believe!"

Far away one could hear the call of the muezzin. Tariq got up slowly, reluctantly. He said, cutting his syllables:

"You-are-not-ti-red-any-more-now, are-you?"

"No," she whispered. "Oh no, master."

"Do you think you will be able to wait till the next time . . . let's say at noon?"

"Yes," she said in one breath, "I will wait."

Suddenly she took his member into her hands, joined like a cup, licked it, drank the semen that still escaped to the last drop. It tasted good. From her toes to the roots of her hair, she felt overwhelmed with gratitude. She closed her eyes and spoke very quickly:

"Please forgive me."

"Aha. Why?"

"I have my menses."

"So?"

"I feel impure."

"Impure! Just wait till the noon day prayer and you will see. Wait with all your juice. Don't wash. And you needn't say any prayers whatsoever. Should I tell you? The blood of the menses is what is most pure on earth. In Islam, there is no constraint! This is what I, Tariq, believe. Or else I am not a Muslim."

He performed his ablutions in a basin fashioned of woven rope, then said his first prayer of the day. From here to nightfall, there would be three others. As a sincere believer, he said them all. Before each of them, he lay with a woman and gave her his male seed. Earthly concerns first, then heaven! This nubile girl was the most beautiful gift the governor of Ifriqiyya, Moussa ibn Moussaïr, had bestowed on him. Her name was Oum-Hakim and she was of tender age, full of ardor and warmth, seventeen springs . . .

His prayer accomplished, he calmly murmured:

"Amen!"

He saluted humanity to the right, then to the left and without transition, he asked:

"Oum-Hakim, if you want your freedom, I will free you this very hour."

She broke out into peals of laughter, a laughter as fresh as the morning dew. She prostrated herself, but not in the direction of Mecca, but in front of the man. With closed eyes, she recited:

"Lord and master, master and Lord.

In my next life, I will not ask to be born a human.

I simply would like to be with you, like

two birds uniting their wings or

two branches entwining their bows . . . "

She sobbed twice, slow, heart-breaking sobs. Tariq Bnou Ziyyad did not comfort her with a caress, he did not even look at her. He said:

"In four hours, you will make love again. Four hours is not very long, is it?"

He tied the laces of his sandals, rose and went down to the harbor to inspect his vessels. Tomorrow at dawn, he would set sail for Spain. Three thousand Berbers, six Arabs. And Oum-Hakim. By herself, she was the triumph of God's glory!

4

Two seasons earlier, in the valley of the Warka, between the high plains and the foothills of the Atlas. A little village of ochre and sienna-colored houses, carved into the side of the mountain, right on the rock. Flat roofs, terraces and slopes covered with dry and the shoots of young grass, cattle grazing greedily. Ruby-red cows with white spots, honey-colored calves tottering on their long legs, goats and kids as black as the children of the Sudan. Up on the edge of the cliffs, play-ful ibex, gazelles and rock squirrels jumped around in pairs. Spread over the entire valley, a carpet of flowers in shades of blue, green, saffron yellow, luxuriant flowers. Clear and rich the bronze and silver voices of springs rose from the mountains. It was the middle of the day, in the heart of springtime. It was peaceful, absolute silence. Not a human being for miles around.

Suddenly, as if coming from another world, a dark rider appeared on the horizon. His beard was black, his head shone blue. He seemed to be one with his dark horse. For a moment, he remained still as a rock. Shielding his eyes with his hand, he studied, scrutinized all that separated him from the other horizon. And all of a sudden, a frantic gallop, where man and his horse were but one, riding with the speed of the desert wind—a wild ride that overcame peace and space with one long, dark dash, hammering hooves moving straight towards the village. Instantly, in one movement, the horse stood still on his four hooves, while the rider dismounted, sat down in the grass. Speaking to the granite wall across from him, he called in a strong voice:

"I am Tariq, son of Ziyyad. I am listening."

The echoes and the reverberations of the echo were his only answer. Slowly, silence fell once more. Some minutes went by or some lustrums. Then, an old man came out of one of the houses. He was as wrinkled as a cypress, his body stout and vigorous. With heavy steps he approached Tariq, turned all around him, bent over and scrutinized his face like a cattle dealer. He said:

"I am Hajgar, chief of the great tribe of the Snassen. I am listening to you."

Tariq did not change his expression. He never changed it thereafter, all day long. Holding himself straight, he said, without raising his voice:

"Hajgar, chief of the great tribe of the Snassen, what do you propose to me?"

Hajgar breathed through his nostrils, and as fast as an arrow he replied:

"And you there, what do you propose to me?"

"If we are going to repeat one another's words like two baboons, I might as well get on my horse and leave at once. I have no time to lose bowing and scraping and talking nonsense."

"Sit back down, my son."

"I have not moved at all. And I am not your son."

"Grouchy, aren't you? Stinker! Nothing or nobody frightens you from what I can see?"

"What does that mean, to be frightened?" asked Tariq, pretending his teeth were shattering.

"Aren't you afraid to die?"

"What's that, to die?"

"You are just as I have been told!" Hajgar concluded laughing. "A real mangy old hide."

Unexpectedly, he made a gesture of peace, holding out both arms, palms open, to his interlocutor, saying sincerely and wearily:

"I want peace."

"I want something other than peace," Tariq Bnou Ziyyad replied. "I want more than peace, something going further than peace. My eyes are already there, one or two centuries ahead. I want all the harvests, all the fruit of peace. Without reneging or perjury, either from you or me. Irreversibly. For you, for me, for your people and mine, as well as for the children yet to be born and for the descendants of our descendants. Is that clear?"

Silence. Phalange after phalange, Hajgar cracked his fingers. Then he spoke in a disillusioned voice:

"I have heard your words and stored them in my head. This abundance of tomorrow that you are talking about, I really want to believe in it . . . let us say, tomorrow. Later, a long time after I will have left this life. Let us say too, that I am concerned about the fate of my tribe and therefore would like nothing better than to believe you now, right away. In that case, can you show me even a single grain of the seed that will, according to you, change the enemy into a brother and war into peace? Hey?"

He put his head forward as if listening to spring. Tariq smiled for the first time. It was a smile without malice, very slow, very patient.

He said with great kindness:

"Give me your hand, brother!"

"All the conquerors are the same," the Berber chief went on, suddenly upset, his face like putty. "They come with outstretched hands, but in them, there is a deathly weapon. As for promises, they only make them if they are faced with a big enemy. They are stuffed full of promises, swollen with them, so much they come out of their seven orifices like wind. Is that what you are doing now? Making promises like the wind?"

"Give me your hand," repeated General Tariq. (His voice was low, a combination of vinegar and honey. His eyes did not blink once.) "What if you and I played a game of arm-wrestling?"

The two men were silent. Tariq Bnou Ziyyad gave the chief time to sit down, as much time as a thrown-off rider would have needed to get back into the saddle. Then he said:

"You are twice as big as I am, three or four times stronger, if I am not mistaken. There should not be any doubt as to who will win."

If the man from the mountain was dumbfounded it was only for a moment. Sitting on his behind like a bear, he shook with silent laughter, full of intense disdain. He said:

"I did not know that the commander in chief of the Islamic army was a boy."

"It is true," the commander admitted in a humble voice. "Sometimes I am having a little fun, especially if my adversaries are not serious people."

His elbow on the ground, his arm stretched out, he added in a low voice:

"Try."

The hand that seemed to tease him was fragile and tiny. Hajgar could easily have squashed it, broken it between his thumb and forefinger. But he told himself that this conqueror had not come from such a distance to have his hand broken, knowing what he was doing. This must hide a trap, the ruse of a fox. He tensed all of his muscles, gripped Tariq's hand as in a vise, nailed it to the ground without stopping to breathe and . . . found himself executing a pirouette, then flying through the air and landing on his back. Time was born, lived and died.

"How did you do it? How?"

Hajgar panted like bellows, his eyes protruding from his face.

"It was nothing," Tariq answered. "I did not do anything, I used your strength, that's all."

He helped Hajgar to his feet, kissed him on the left shoulder. Then he launched into a blazing speech, as if his words were flames, and they sounded all the more brutal because his eyes remained calm, shiny and full of kindness.

"If only one atom of what is in my heart were thrown upon this mountain, it would melt."

Looking Hajgar straight into the eyes he said, bitterly:

"This war has lasted thirty years, a continuous back and forth of killing, incessant pursuits from Tripoli to the Atlantic Ocean and vice-versa. Sometimes we win, sometimes you do. Very well! At that rate, in one or two generations, not a single Berber will be left, not a single Arab. I want the contrary: that is my mission."

"All I want is your hide," Hajgar replied quietly. "Poor innocent! Here you are on my territory, all alone, unarmed. You might as well say naked and plucked like a chicken. Hah!"

"Hah!" repeated Tariq Bnou Ziyyad like an echo. "The poor innocent suggests you look up. Look!"

High up, encircling the valley, archers, one knee on the ground, bows flexed to the breaking point. Behind each one of them, blowing steam through their nostrils, a horse, as still as a statue.

"They will do nothing but what Destiny has preordained," said Tariq in a calm voice.

"It's a trap!" Hajgar cried. His face had turned liver-colored.

"No. An elementary precaution. During the past weeks and months, the messengers of your people have met with mine. They have negotiated, palavered till their tongues were sore and their spittle dried up, in order to prepare my coming here, to this meeting with History.

Did you imagine even for one moment that I would have risked throwing myself into the lion's mouth with nothing but Islam inside me and the Koran tucked under my arm? If the human word, be it ever so noble, does not carry, it is enough to have an arrow precede it and it will enter the most obtuse brain. So I am asking you, who is the plucked chicken, you or I?"

"I am," Hajgar replied with a mixture of rage and bitter resignation. "A little while ago, you spoke of peace through arms, did you not? How do you want my submission, dead or alive?"

"I have no use for a conquered man," General Tariq said loud and clear. "Even less for a corpse. You are neither one or the other. I need what you have left to live with, the essential: your youth, no matter how old you are."

He snapped his fingers, and instantly the archers disappeared. Their mounts as well. It was as if they had never been there.

"I need the strength of your people," he continued, stressing each syllable. "I need its valor, its honor, the best its hands can produce and the best of their tongues. Do you have anything to propose to me that resembles the fire of life?"

The tribal chief looked intently to the two horizons, contemplated the radiant sky above his head, the ground he sat on. From his innermost depths, like from the profundity of his most distant past, a strange feeling with the silvery sound of a spring arose in him. His heart was swollen with emotion, his throat tight, when he said slowly, word for word, in a low voice:

"Speak. Now I am listening to you."

"It was about time."

"I said: now I am listening to you."

Tariq nodded, rubbed his hands as if he were going to do his ablutions.

"By God!" he called out. "By His glory! Another general could have been named in my place and he might not have deigned to stop to talk with you. But Destiny has decreed that it should be I. Those who have come before me, have only shown me the way. I have no desire to conquer your territory, not a single slope of the Maghreb. It would be very little compared to what I intend to accomplish."

"Speak," Hajgar repeated. "Explain what I am beginning to understand and which is beyond me."

Tariq pointed to the north with his outstretched arm. With a faraway look he said:

"I am going over there, to the other side of the White Middle Sea, the Mediterranean. Over there, I have already won the victory without even setting foot on the shore. Simply because I wish it. Over there, I will found the Oumma, the Islamic community where all members will be equal, in fact and by law. To do this, I need the best men, because the Oumma will replace the ties of blood, the clans and even the families. Those who will join me in my venture, conquerors and the humiliated of yesterday, I will make them proud again, so help me God. Proud and triumphant. History crosses your path. You have a choice: to rise and march with it, or to remain sitting."

For a long time, Hajgar scrutinized the general's eyes. A wave of hope washed over him, removing his last doubts.

"Will we be obliged," he asked, "to abandon our traditions and to convert to Islam?"

"No."

"Who guaranties it?"

"Islam."

"Which Islam?"

"The Islam that I am, in the flesh."

Hajgar stood up.

"I will give you two thousand warriors. And what warriors! Bani Snassens. You know them, hey?"

"I know them," the commander-in-chief replied. "But I am not asking for that much. I am offered soldiers from all over the globe. And monkeys, you have some in your tribe from what I have been told?"

"Our watchmen? Hah, they live in the trees. They can tell a shadow from a shadow in the darkest night, hahah!"

"How many are there?"

"Difficult to say . . . Wait a minute . . . thirty-two, perhaps thirty-four . . . Some have not come down from the trees since your presence was signalled in the area, one territory from here."

"Those are the ones I need. The land of the Visigoths is covered with forests. I will wage the war in the trees. And what do you have to offer me for the building of the Oumma? I am listening."

Hajgar lounged into a long tirade about the million of years old virtues of the Berber peoples, their customs, their laws. Tariq listened carefully. He spoke with kindness:

"Time grinds the words, scatters their ashes. To whom do these cows over there belong?"

Taken aback, the tribal chief turned around, smiled from one ear to the other.

"They belong to us," he said proudly. You will not find any like them for ten parasangs around."

"That's true," the general agreed. I have never seen such beauties, by God and His glory. I can already see their offspring, heifers and calves grazing in the country I will conquer. I want those cows. They too will belong to the Oumma of tomorrow."

Without any transition he added:

"When I was given my command, I at once cleaned up the army. I only kept those able to be victorious. Once peace is established, these same warriors will build the new society. I selected only the best. I expect that you will do the same with your tribe, if you want to follow me. By Allah, the Almighty, no son of Adam shall enter my kingdom who is motivated by thoughts of profit or lust for power. Prune among your people, no matter how close they are to you. Cut off the dead wood."

Hajgar bent down, tore out a tuft of grass and began to chew it slowly. After he thought for a long time, he said:

"What you are asking is difficult, indeed, impossible. Those who elected me chief are chiefs in their own right. Their clans are related since the night of time and, in each clan there are sub-clans. I could graze all the grass in this valley before two of them could agree in their palavers. If you shake one of them, the whole tribe tumbles down."

Tariq was silent. He waited.

"I need time, a lot of time. I have to think and think again. And in the end, who knows? Maybe it is I who will be thrown over."

General Tariq Bnou Ziyyad cleared his throat. A slight smile crinkled his nose like a fox's.

"In that case, he said, you leave your tribe and come alone. Go and call the next one. Go!"

o o o

All day long the delegations followed one another. The Ancients of the tribes of Zaer, Zenata, Lawata, Bani Mellil, Aït Yafelman . . . Some among them came from far away, from the Souss and even from the territory of the Barqa, behind the Atlas mountains. All had answered the call of History. They were eager to see the man in the flesh who, instead of making war, had sent them messengers only to invite them to a meeting in the valley of the Warka.

Tariq received them separately, despite their efforts to speak to him with several voices, according to the ancestral customs. He had only two ears to listen to them, as equals—and only one tongue to direct them in a few words. The goal he had set for himself a long time ago was to isolate each man from the influence of his clan and let him speak for himself. It was his old tactic of the Bedouin, son of the desert: in the immense silence between the sky and the mountains and faced with the smiling aloofness of his interlocutor, a tribal chief, having arrived full of his own importance, no matter how determined he was, could not but break the silence which suddenly surrounded him, with a flood of words. And this torrent of words was already a defeat.

As an army general, Tariq Bnou Ziyyad then used a second strategy. He was more than affable. His face and his whole comportment showed only meekness. Sincerely, his eyes kind, he told his hosts:

"I am your guest. You are a man of wisdom and of experience. Grant me your counsel, help me. What can you propose to me. I am listening to you."

And without fail, he listened carefully. From time to time he nodded earnestly, closed his eyes as if to fully comprehend all that was told to him, down to the slightest details, then he would approve by blinking an eyelid, smile more broadly and concluded with these words:

"I have heard you. And now, here are my suggestions. They are the basis—there is no other—of the whole discussion. Either you march with History—and I am History—or else you get back into the hole of your past. In that case, call the next one."

The man remained seated, compromising at once with a resolution he had believed to be irrevocable. There was always a way to come to an understanding with a fox. At night fall, at the general assembly of the Ancients which had gradually formed around him, Tariq repeated word for word what this one here and that one over there (and in front of everybody he pointed them out with his finger) had said to him when they had been alone, man to man, with their tongue and their honor. Always, in all circumstances had he acted thus: confront people with their words while waiting for their acts to follow.

Late at night, at the light of burning torches, they voted by counting the held-up hands. A pact of non-aggression and of mutual assistance was concluded between them and him at the end of negotiations as deep as the roots of the crab grass, based (at least as far as he was concerned), on a willingness to refuse. These were his ultimate tactics: to get what he wanted, he left no doubt that he could break any agreement.

o o o

They celebrated the occasion with the feast of feasts: the *boundouk*, the ancestor of couscous, a giant kettle in which a whole sheep had slowly simmered, giving off the juice of its meat, its bones and its innards; half-way through the cooking, vegetables had been added and some spices only the mountain people knew, a harmonious choice of what grew under the ground and what grew above, in the proper portions to add to the juice of the sheep. And now, cut in quarters, the steaming innards on top, the meat was served on a huge platter, carved from the wood of the argan tree and two men's steps wide.

Two other platters just as gigantic contained the vegetables and a mound of green barley grains, tender, picked just before they were ripe, and that dozens of women's hands had steamed over a charcoal fire spread on a lattice work made of doum palms. Accompanied by the sounds of drums, flutes and cymbals the echoes of which could be heard from hill top to hill top, they religiously formed a ball of *boundouk* out of vegetables and a piece of meat, moistened it with a ladle of broth and then chewed it with a silent prayer to Mother Earth who nourished them, their eyes swimming, nostrils quivering with pleasure.

Savouring the dishes in small portions, first inhaling their fragrance, Tariq Bnou Ziyyad murmured "Allah! Allah!" with each mouthful. He thought of the unmentionable food the Arabs consumed with delight, like those small balls made of crushed camel hair held together with blood. To boil water or milk, they simply threw in a red-hot stone from the fire . . . Sons of Islam, he never stopped to marvel at Providence who had arranged Islam to be born among them. Truly, if there was a civilization, it was here, in this heathen country. He would carry the memory of this succulent dish away in his belly and would bring it to honors in the Andalusian palaces of tomorrow.

He saddled his horse and left at dawn. With him galloped the new era. With every stride, the great design became clearer, acquired greater force, more reality. Everything was now ready to realize the greatest dream of all: these Berbers were not Muslims, not yet; but he, General Tariq Bnou Ziyyad, he was, by God, going to forge them not only into the tip of the lance of his army, but make them into the pillars of the future Oumma . . . a leading class cut off from all ethnic or family ties, severed from all ties of their craft or fortune. These men would exist by their purpose alone, they would rise from obscurity and go back there when they no longer served their purpose.

o o o

At the same time, in the valley of the Warka, precise instructions went out in all imaginable directions. By nightfall they had already crossed over the high Atlas mountains, from mouth to ear crossed the forests of cedars, oaks and pine trees, rushed along the rivers and through the plains with the speed of a wildfire, reached the farthest corners of the Berber country. Every Son of the Land received the order to go, from wherever he might be and search for the ancestor of antique times, Azwaw Aït Yafelman, and to tell him about the meeting with General Tariq. Thus began the greatest human migration the world had ever known.

5

On that same day, at the mouth of the Oum-er-Bia, in a little synagogue carved into the black cliff by generations of hands, Rabbi Eliahou Ba Shiméon slowly unrolled the parchments of the Torah, shook its leaves, then refolded them without having read a single word. His eyes expressionless, he said:

"On this Yom Kippur, I will not sing the Kol Nidra. We will not pronounce the ritualistic oath of the B'rith."

Around his neck, he wore a cord from which a bull's horn was suspended. He took it and blew three long notes that sounded like the three death rattles of an animal. The faithful shivered, heads bent. He said:

"The Eternal has wanted it thus: since the destruction of the temple in Jerusalem, our people have been wandering all over the earth. The ancestors of our tribe found refuge here. The Berbers who took them in offered them help and understanding. They were the Aït Yafelman. They made us obey their laws, but they left us in peace. Then came the Muslim like a sword of fire, from the desert where he was born right to the Atlantic Ocean. His name was Oqba ibn Nafi. This happened thirty years ago. He razed the city of Azemmour to the ground, deported the whole population. Those of my brothers who are old remember that man: to us, he granted our lives. He did not touch a single one of our houses. Thus we were able to safeguard the essential: all the traditions, the knowledge, all the secrets of the Jewish people, we are the ones who have kept them from the most ancient times."

He went from faithful to faithful, caressed their faces with his fingers, using the light touch of a blind man, calling each one by his name. In front of him, behind him, to his right as to his left, people were breathing hard. He said:

"What has been entrusted to us, we have kept safe. Without using it a single time. Waiting for a sign. This sign, I have received a few days ago. It spoke to me clearly. Spoke to me with the voice of another Muslim: General Tariq Bnou Ziyyad. This man is the worthy successor of the Emir Oqba ibn Nafi, because he considers us to be the people of his Book, adoring one unique God. And, at the same time, he far out-distances the emir Oqba by his vision. He unites several desires in this single one: he wants to unite the Berber clans and tribes by ties of the spirit; he wants to gather the sons of Sem, descendants of Isaac and Ismael, in the same undertaking; he wants the heritage of all of our prophets which he affirms to be those of his own religion as well; he wants to conquer an empire in which all members, wherever they may come from, will form but one community;

he wants the best the Creator has created, and the best of what is inside them. That is all he wants. While he spoke to me, his voice remained as calm as a rock. He knows me profoundly. He knows everything about us, all the treasures of industry and knowledge which, inherited from father to son, we have kept hidden since the beginning; one would think he is the devil himself. I have made an alliance with him."

He paused and it was like a break in the religious silence that had greeted his words. He said:

"The waiting has come to an end at last. Tomorrow your women will bake you bread with leaven. We will leave. We will take nothing with us, nothing but what is in our heads. May the Eternal forgive me if I am ready to believe in a rebirth of the Jewish people!"

Thus began the second migration, without doubt the most far-reaching History has ever known.

o o o

Santraj took leave of his family and left the city of Qouds in the Khorassan, a board under his arm his only luggage. It was a square plank with an edge around it, divided into one hundred squares, alternately white and black. In the pockets of his gown he carried figurines, ten black and ten white, each of them representing a number between one and ten. Santraj had a passion for figures (to the great despair of his family who had hoped to make a reader of the Koran of him, even a judge) and he had just resolved the puzzle of arithmetics. He was sure of it. From now on there would be no more need to count on the fingers, or use the abacus or a bundle of sticks cut into different lengths, as the merchants did. The calculating board instantly gave the results of a multiplication or a division, an addition or a subtraction. It sufficed to place the pawns in their proper places and move them according to strict rules, the knight on the bias and jumping three squares, the vizier diagonally, the tower to the right, etc. One could even obtain a geometric progression—this "thing without a name" the clerks of the sultan's court had made fun of when they threw him out. Unquestionably, the Orient had invented everything, even the cult of the unique God, and for that reason, the whole future was set.

A caravan of pilgrims were leaving for Mecca, and Santraj joined them early in the middle of the day. In the holy city he would surely find another caravan going in the direction of the Maghreb al-Aqsa, Morocco, and once he arrived there, he would find a third which would take him even farther, across the sea to this Oumma which was soon to be established. The travellers talked about it so much and with such excitement, that if you believed them, it was already in place and flourishing. Santraj had only recently become a Muslim and was convinced that Islam expected a rather unusual pilgrimage of him: his face turned at the same time to the past and to the future and the four cardinal points.

o o o

Admiral Yannis Emiris, called the limping Satan, had felt the call of the wind. Departing from Aegina in the Ionian sea, he headed full speed towards the straights of Calpé. On board his squadron of triremes, he had the most experienced sailors of the Mediterranean—and a full cargo of arms and *naft*, this Greek fire that caused terrific damages in a naval battle. He was going to offer his men and the weapons to the conqueror along with his knowledge of navigation and devilish strategies which had given him his cruel reputation. He was even willing to embrace the religion of Allah in all sincerity, as long as it brought him power and glory. This General Tariq they talked about in the harbors in four or five different languages was after all only a Bedouin, son of his faith and not of his deeds. He, Yannis Emiris, was the result of what he had accomplished since his long-ago adolescence: naval war. He also knew how to listen patiently, make people like him. He was able to understand people, to penetrate their thoughts and to foresee their secret reactions and their hidden desires. Thus he had eliminated many of his adversaries.

Standing like a masthead figure in the forecastle deck of his admiral's ship, Yannis Emiris smiled coldly. He was wet with spray and crowned with foam. The stern cut the waves into two long, sparkling sprays of water, which seemed to him like a border of banners that from wave to wave brought him closer to this man of great distinction he saw surge from the high seas: Admiral Younès, the emir of the sea.

6

Standing on the headland of Calpé in front of his three thousand warriors who formed a semi-circle, Tariq Bnou Ziyyad shouted a verse of the Koran at the top of his lungs, followed without any transition by a resounding order:

"God is sufficient unto himself: He does not need the earth's help. Take out your swords."

Three thousand swords glistened in the rising sun.

"Break them! Throw the pieces into the sea. And now, climb up into the trees. Your sling shots and your slip knots will be ample from here to Cordoba. When we arrive, I will count the survivors."

o o o

Half-way to Cordoba, they told him that the Arabs had landed in Spain, that everywhere whole families were going ashore, horses, camels and carts. He said:

"All the better."

He broke into laughter. He said:

"They will occupy the territory to the last tuft of grass, I know them. And then, they are the best horsemen in the world. As long as they gallop, the enemy will not dream of attacking our rear. Nothing resists their passion, nothing and no one."

He did not add, although he kept it constantly in mind, that the real problems would not arise until peace time. How to transform these nomads into sedentary people and make them live peaceably in the same city, under the same banner. All would depend on the men already there. They would have to be very tolerant and at the same time, very strong.

"Chief, the special envoy of Emir Moussa ibn Noussaïr, the governor of North Africa, wishes to see you. He is here, waiting for you, covered with dust and impatience."

"Aha, he wants to see me?"

The strong man is not he who makes use of his strength, but he who dominates his anger, taught a hadith of the Prophet. Tariq took a deep breath, his mouth open. He said:

"Here is my answer: I will not receive him, I have no time to lose. Let him go and tell his master and the Caliph, his master's master that they will get their share of the cake. The whole cake. They can have the glory all to themselves. It will be their victory, not mine. They will have the spoils, the gold, the precious stones, the slaves, the beautiful captives, everything they dream about in the name of Islam! We have hardly started our march and here they are already, the vultures and the jackals, each watching the other jealously, not wanting him around. This is how they divided and destroyed the Oumma of the East. May God the All Powerful grant me several lives to achieve my task. *Bismaillahi rahmani rahim!*"

The Berber soldier looked and listened, his face tense. Never had he seen his commander-in-chief so upset. To conclude the matter he suggested:

"Would it not be best if I went to strangle the special envoy right now. And if his master comes around, I will strangle him too. I have a good rope, look. What do you think, chief?"

"No," Tariq said. Time will take care of them."

He added furiously:

"What are you waiting for to get going?"

"Julien, the Nazarene is asking for an audience, chief."

"Aha? He too is joining the rush for the spoils?"

"I tied him up while awaiting your orders, chief. He was loaded with arms. One never knows . . . "

"A renegade who wanted to square accounts with his sovereign, King Rodrigue of Spain. Governor of the straits and its two naval bases, Ceuta and Algésiras, he had transported Tariq's troops across the sea at night. To show his faith in the commander-in-chief of the Islamic army, he had given him his two daughters as hostages.

"The dog. I have burned his ships and he still has not understood. God does not love traitors. Neither do I."

"Can I strangle him then?" the Berber asked eagerly.

"Go ahead."

A five-man delegation arrived with a strong escort. Tariq Bnou Ziyyad spoke to the most important looking one among them. He said:

"Before you open your mouth, open your ears. I am a conqueror, that is true. But a conqueror in love with peace. That is why I have come to your country and went as far as Cordoba, then Toledo and farther yet: to bring peace there. Sit down, the others can remain standing. Control your tongue and your words and tell me only the essential of what your king Rodrigue wants."

He leaned against a tree, hands joined and had a quiet nap while the Spaniard spoke. When he reopened his eyes, it was to give an order to his guards:

"Cut him to pieces."

They cut him to pieces in front of his horrified companions. They boned him, threw away the head, the tripes and his innards, the hands and feet. They carried the meat away on their shoulders, bloody and still steaming, to go and cook it a little distance away in a clearing. A long time later, they came back with a huge kettle (a *guedra*), sat down in a circle and said all together: "Bismillah! In the name of the Lord!" And they began to eat without speaking, intent on their pleasure. They clicked their jaws, strands of saliva dripping from the corners of their lips and their eyes turning redder and redder. They took turns gulping the sauce. A Berber with his tongue hanging out, lapped up the rest from the bottom of the kettle, making gurgling noises. They burped, rubbed their stomachs and gave thanks to the Creator:

"*Alhamdou lillah!* Praise be to God."

Tariq recited the prayer for the dead. He had taken part in the feast and felt revived. Out of the corner of his eye, he watched the four remaining men of the delegation, and they could do nothing but look at him. They had had time to die a thousand deaths, to hope against hope, to turn green and grey, to vomit and lose control of their bowels. Tariq remained still for a long moment. Finally he told them in a conversational tone:

"We have eaten enough. You may leave. After what your departed comrade has told me, your king expects an answer to his peace proposal. Go and bring it to him. You have seen it with your own eyes."

Not one of them moved, had the strength to move. The general's voice became softer, smoother.

"Did you know that Muslims get hungry again very quickly?"

They got up. They got up with tottering legs and went off with scared little steps, looking behind them as if they could not yet believe in their salvation. At the edge of the forest, they began to run, crying and sobbing. Silence fell. And then an orchestra of laughter rose amidst the silence.

"Who has kitchen duty today?" Tariq asked.

"I have," said Hawch.

"Step forward."

Hawch took a few steps, knelt down close enough to receive a cuff on the ear.

"Satisfactory," the commander-in-chief said to him. "Quite satisfactory. But you put in too many onions. If I did not have such a sensitive palate, I would have thought I was eating human flesh. One could hardly taste the mutton."

The laughter turned into yapping, then died down.

"What did you do with the flesh of the Christian?"

"Well," said Hawch, rolling his eyes, "I threw it out down there, piece by piece. Perhaps I should have put it in a bag and salted it, in case our supplies got low, hey, Chief?"

"Go and collect the pieces. And while you are at it, get this head and the rest out of my sight. Dig a grave and bury the corpse. That man had a soul and the soul is immortal. God has said:

We shall assemble your bones from where ever they are scattered. We shall revive you. Do you know any suras of the Koran?"

"Oh yes, Chief. So, so. The short ones."

"Recite the shortest over the grave. He has just rendered a great service to our cause. His companions are now spreading the horrible news all over: the Muslims are cannibals! At present the population is fleeing as fast as their legs can carry them. And so perhaps, we will enter into an empty city of Cordoba."

"You are as sly as the most Berber of Berbers among us."

"I am a Berber," said Tariq Bnou Ziyyad.

Hawch bent down and kissed his feet.

o o o

A detachment of armed Bedouins brought the message and handed it to Tariq personally when his army was two days' march away from Cordoba. It almost made him lose his momentum and his faith. In threatening terms, the emir Moussa ibn Noussaïr reminded him that he was his military superior in all things and that he, son of Ziyyad, was only his "vassal", a military servant whose only task it was to carry out orders strictly. If he had entrusted him with the expedition into Spain, it had been only to open the road to the undersigned, governor of Ifriquiyya and personal friend of the Commander of the Faithful, may God keep him, and not to take any initiatives himself. By Allah and the Prophet, what was this war fought at night . . . and in the trees like wildcats or the savages of the *jahiliya*, the time of ignorance? Islam had nothing to hide, it was the light of lights! Its soldiers had always fought by day, face to face with the enemy. If they had to die, even to the last one, well, they would be martyrs who would inspire the fresh troops, and there was no lack of those. This was the first point. Second, all battles fought by Islam had up-to-now been fought by horsemen, sabres drawn. Order was hereby given to the addressee to let these monkeys with human faces do menial tasks and to leave the rest to the horsemen. Last and most important: the nobles were to have priority in entering Cordoba and to celebrate the victory there and take command in the name of those entitled to it. Then came some insults, greetings in poetic Arabic —and an invocation of the Lord of the worlds, *amen.*

Post-scriptum: The subaltern of the emir was not to proceed further than Cordoba. New instructions would be issued him at the appropriate time, God willing.

Tariq Bnou Ziyyad calmly ate the official letter. Just as calmly he revised his threatened plans, took the city by assault at the projected date, carried on to Toledo from where he chased King Rodrigue at the head of his army, killed him, pursued and exterminated the fugitives for three days, and then retraced his steps, triumphant, but empty. For him, the war was over, or just about. Another one was beginning, the extent of which he had not foreseen, more murderous and more absurd. This war was between the two conquerors themselves. And this war, he could neither stop nor win, unless he possessed the force of Destiny.

7

Standing on the ramparts overlooking Cordoba, the hills and the Guadalquivir, Tariq Bnou Ziyyad contemplated the shining waters of the river. And it was as if all the autumns of the world died and that at the same time, all the springtimes of the world were born in him. Six months had passed since the conquest of the city.

Oum-Hakim was in his arms. Suddenly she stiffened.

"Are you cold, master?"

"Go inside."

"You are not cold, master?"

"Go inside and wait for me."

She went with small, graceful steps, looking over her shoulder, her eyes fearful and fluid at the same time. Lieutenant Boutr did not deign look at her. He scrutinized his commander's face with horror.

"You are not dying, chief?"

"Boutr, the most faithful among the faithful!" Tariq said slowly. He caressed his head.

"You are not going to die, are you?"

"I am still alive."

"Is your soul sick?"

"No. Not really. I would have liked . . . I would have liked to make my entrance into this city as . . . as I had dreamed about so much . . ."

Across space, thirty years earlier, down there in the Maghreb-Aqsa, the legendary emir Oqba ibn Nafi and his riders had reached the borders of the Atlantic Ocean, filled with joy. All of them had dismounted, sobbing with happiness, and suddenly very humble before the immensity of creation. Then there was the birth. After that came the breath. Frail, bare-headed, breathing like bellows, the emir Oqba ibn Nafi had entered the sea until the waves reached the breast plate of his mount. And it was here, with the water rising under him as emotion rose within him, that he said his prayers of thanksgiving. It was here, in the tides of the Ocean that he unfurled the green banner of the Prophet. Behind him, on the beach and for miles around, deep silence. Conquerors and conquered were silent. This was at the mouth of the Oum-er-Bia in the city of Azemmour. Not a single drop of blood had been shed, as if the beginning of the new world had happened without any pain whatsoever, neither of body or spirit. And perhaps Islam was young then, young and pure, with everything to hope for, everything to love . . .

The water. Thirty years later, General Tariq, successor and ardent admirer of Oqba ibn Nafi, looked at the green and peaceful Guadalquivir. Time had calmed the river, washed it of all impurities. Tariq still saw it, red with blood, chopped off heads floating in its stream.

When they attacked, the Bedouin troops had suddenly become wild hordes again, out of control, destroying everything under their hooves. Their horses, rising on their hindlegs, smashed facades, doors, people. Sounds of Gehenna. Wild yells of victory between heaven and earth. Death rattles of those who had been trampled, stabbed, had their throats cut. They vied with each other as to who could destroy the most, kill the greatest number of infidels, as if they were trying to convince themselves that they were blind instruments of a blind Providence. Immediately there followed the frantic ransacking of the city. Carpets woven of gold threads and covered with emeralds were cut into pieces with an axe to make them easier to carry. The jewel of the highest Antiquity, Solomon's table, had its legs broken off, its jewels pried from it. Even the rafters of the roofs came crashing down. After all, they needed a wood fire to cook their food. Even the straying cats were killed with cross-bows and stones, gutted while they were still warm, filled with rubies and diamonds and sewn together. They were thrown away to be picked up later on the run. The chiefs would surely control the spoils—one fifth for them according to custom, the rest to be shared among the warriors. Thirst for power, glory of possession. Galley slaves, if there were any, and Tariq's Berber troops crossed the upheaval wielding their whips and came back to report to their chief, battered and voiceless . . .

"Are you still heartsick, chief?" Boutr asked.

"Give me your coat," Tariq said.

He wrapped himself in it, pulled the hood over his head and sat down. He said:

"Lord of the worlds, You know better than I do that this was not my war. This city You see here at Your feet, I could have entered it without any violence, using ruse instead as in all of my battles, at night, by the river, under the water. I had prepared a Berber detachment, who are specialists in this matter, just for this purpose: the Aït Yafelman, Sons of the Water. Another section, the Zenata, would have climbed over the ramparts at the same hour. And You know better than I do, Lord, that these devils of Zenatas are able to climb the smoothest and the highest wall with nothing to help them but their thumbs and the soles of their feet. I had chosen the best warriors."

He prostrated himself, forehead to the ground. He continued:

"Lord of the worlds, in the Book, You have clearly asked the question which has always haunted humanity: *Is it possible that, when we have returned to dust, we become a new creation?* Erasing our doubts, You have said: *The semen with which you beget children, did you create it or did We?* Six months have passed since this carnage took place and men's souls were possessed by the devil—and it has always been Your word that upheld me. Six months during which I used all my resources, day after day, night after night, all my cunning, to channel the force of the conquerors from destruction to rebuilding, from death to life. I saw the moment when Islam, hardly arrived in Spain, was going to turn this country into a desert and itself into nothingness. This is why I have broken so many backs. I made your believers compete even for the smallest task of digging. Counting on their pride, I called on strangers and the conquered of yesterday to give them an example and show perseverance. It was a failure too. I brought their families over down to the last cousin, I brought their cantors and their bards to sing their praises. And their *neffars, nays, gheitas* and other musical instruments so they would have one continuous feast and not feel cut off from their roots. I had them carried along with themselves, such as they are. I made each one of them feel that he was irreplaceable. And now, Lord, listen to them build the world of tomorrow."

He stopped shivering. Tense and rigid under his cloak, he seemed to be listening all of a sudden.

"Are you satisfied, Lord? Not I. Not at all. If I am a believer, I am also astute. My eyes are wide open, no veil covers them. They see no mirage. I want to look reality in the face and not be misled by words. I believe in You, but I have no illusions about those You have created. That is my strength and my torment. My solitude. Help me. Enlighten me. Appease me. And if Your will be done, You should be aware of how things are. I am wandering. We are all wandering. Lead us onto the right path. And first of all, tell us where this right path is."

He did not bother to order his thoughts before pronouncing them, but threw them up to the sky as if with the help of a catapult, with all the passion that had always lived within him. Sincere and ardent he said:

"You ask too much of us, Lord! Too much and all at the same time. After all, we are only bipeds, blessed with sense and nonsense, coherent in our faith and disintegrated in this same faith, capable of the highest deeds and the most extreme cruelty. Yes, You ask too much of us! It is like asking us to build a house and to begin with the roof. And we don't even have foundations worthy of that name. Those we have at the moment consist of sand and wind. We are still too fragile, fragile and vain, for Islam to rest on our shoulders. Give us time, Lord, to grow into rocks. You were there when they took this city, You saw it all. What weight did the Koran carry compared to the prehistoric instincts that suddenly invaded the conquerors? And they acted in Your name! . . . How is it possible that, inspired by Islam, Your servants could have acted with such cruelty? *Those* were Muslims? I am telling you, that it will take a century or two to change these looters into believers. Who guaranties me that, in one or two generations, they will not become the strangers they were in the beginning—and that . . . and that our future will not be the religion of the past? How many lives will we need, how many oceans of faith and mountains of patience, how much skin of our teeth and sweat of our souls, before we will reach, one day, at last, the state of human beings motivated by greater humanity? Do You really believe, Lord, that the predators that we are, thirsting for domination, and I tell You, I am the first, will turn into angels from one day to the next by your grace alone, ready to fly to the aid of the orphan, the widow, the stranger, ready to right the wrongs, to establish justice, to apply Your laws, to practice love as the basis for society—and especially, especially to share the *worldly goods* with those neglected by fate. I don't believe it. Not at all. I will perhaps believe it in one or two centuries, when Your word will have entered their skull and become one with their blood. You know better than I do, Lord, that the Prophet needed an iron hand besides the Message he projected in front of their eyes like a goal to strive for. When he died, those who had been violently opposed to him, the Korïchites of Mecca, well, they succeeded him. They converted, of course. But at present, it is they who have the power and rule the Empire. Glory, truth and money. This is where we stand now while I am speaking to you. I had thought that in turning my back on the Orient, the old world, I would create an 'Oumma' free of all blemish. I am not a prophet, but neither am I a fool. This is why I humbly ask you to grant my prayer: prolong my life by a century or two, You who transcend the borders of eternity. In one or two centuries, I will finally be able to enter Cordoba. I will see the true establishment of Islam, not a dream or a desire. I will be nothing but emotion then. My venerated Islamic master, the emir Oqba ibn Nafi, celebrated Your creation in the sea. As for me, I will celebrate those You created. I will proclaim Your glory, Oh Lord of the universe, God of all mankind! And little will it matter to me if You receive me in Your paradise, for I will have built it myself, during my lifetime, with these very hands!"

He chanted aloud:

"We have come from You and we return to You, Lord. In Your hands You hold the kingdom. You are the kingdom! As You have proclaimed in the Koran, You have created life and death in order to make of us Your best creation—of us, the human beings. Take away our doubts, Lord. Forgive us our trespasses, past and future. Let us persevere. Grant some of your noble spirit to the animals that we are. Cure us from our worldly hunger and thirst which makes us so small compared to what we might be and do. The door that leads to You and to ourselves is so narrow. Bless us, Lord! Let us live not according to our ideas, but according to our hearts, our hands, this spark of light you have laid into our eyes. Let Islam succeed here and now and not after our deaths in an hereafter we know nothing about."

He said "Amen!" and rose. He rose and saw Boutr's ashen face, his wide-open eyes. He bent over the ramparts and looked at what his lieutenant was looking at.

Lit torches smoking in full daylight. A dense, silent crowd. In front of the crowd, a camel, a camel colt and a very old man, tiny, insignificant looking. The animals and the people stood motionless. His head lifted toward the sky, the old man looked at Tariq Bnou Ziyyad with a sharp eagle eye. A long, intense moment passed. And suddenly, it was as if time was torn apart, swallowing the present—this eternal present moment that encloses life, no matter how grandiose and turned toward the future human ventures might be. Tariq asked himself *who* was tired, old and frightened. From down below the old man was still looking at him. And then, he smiled at him with all his wrinkles as if he had finally found the face of a friend after many years of separation.

Tariq shook himself, took a deep breath, chased his sad thoughts. But still he felt ice-cold pin pricks needle his spine.

"Does this old carcass know me?" he asked Boutr abruptly.

Boutr stood still as a rock. His eyes riveted on the man with the camel, he said in an odd, toneless voice:

"He . . . he has . . . he has come back!"

"Does he know me?" the general repeated.

When Boutr turned his face toward his chief, it reflected joy, veneration, fear. He had to make several starts before he could speak, his voice changing from low to high pitch:

"All of us. He knows all of us. The living and the dead. He knows each of us by name. He knows our past. What we lived through. What we might have lived through. The good about us as well as the bad. The skeleton that is buried under the earth and the skeleton we will become one day. He has the time of times. Some say he is of my tribe, the Aït Yafelman. His name is Azwaw Aït Yafelman. But he died a long time ago. And here he is back, and it is completely natural. Some say he is the Son of the Land, the ancestor of the ancient people. But all of us believe that he is the Master of the Hand. His hand can resuscitate the dead, his hand can do anything."

He fell silent as if all life had gone out of him, as if in his confusion he had betrayed a secret. Tariq went up to him, looked him up and down and said:

"Take your coat back, lieutenant. You will need it to cover up what is left of your superstitions. You only converted recently to our faith. I did not ask you to preach heathenish stories or to tell legends. I asked the Muslim that you are if this bag of bones knows me."

"He has come from the past century to see you," Boutr answered reluctantly. The words came out of his mouth one by one, dry and sparse. "Yes, he knows your name and your past."

"How do you know?" the general cried. "Who told you?"

"*He did.*"

And Boutr pointed to the old man.

"I did not hear him speak. I am not deaf."

"Of course not, chief. He no longer has a tongue. But he continues to speak. That is what he told me."

"What are you talking about? Do I have to clap you into irons?"

"He is speaking to you! I read the words on his lips. Lip-reading is my specialty."

Dizzily Tariq Bnou Ziyyad questioned the rest of irrationality that was left in him—even in him, who represented clearly and purely God's religion that was clear and pure. And irrationality implied the purest faith as well as cruelty sometimes put in the service of that faith. For he himself had been cruel in the preparation of this war and in the way he had waged it, he had to admit. And he intended to remain cruel in peace time until the Kingdom came, without mercy for men and their abdication whatever shape it might take, not because he was a warrior, but because he believed in his inner strength and could not conceive of an Islam that did not measure up to his expectations and its image: without weakness. His face red, he shouted an order to Boutr which was tempting fate.

"Well, go ahead and read! What does he say?"

"He says: read!"

"Then what? What do I have to read, according to him?"

"*Read in the name of your Lord who has created all things; who has created man from an atom . . .*"

Tariq heaved a sigh of relief. He snapped his fingers, thumb against forefinger.

"That's very good," he approved happily. "He knows the first verses, that have been revealed to the Prophet, by heart. But he did not come from so far away to recite me the whole Book, did he? Tell him it is not necessary, that I will make him lecturer of the Koran for the deaf-mutes . . . in one or two centuries when Cordoba will be Cordoba. But you claim he has time?"

Boutr was not pretending not to have heard. He did, in fact, not hear anything. He was all sight. Holding up his hand to shield his eyes against the sun, he carefully followed the movement of Azwaw's lips and translated as he went along.

"Read! Read in the name of the tree. There are roots and there are branches. The branches lose their leaves in the autumn; some of them become dead wood and others are born to replace them, nourished with the sap that always rises from the roots."

"Wait." Tariq whispered.

He was beginning to understand. This weakling without tongue nor age was not as faint-hearted as he looked. So he was preaching a counter-Koran? And furthermore, he was the ancestor of the ancient people? It did not matter that they were Muslims, these immobile Berbers around him, even Boutr, still believed in him. But, by God and His glory, he was welcome! He would be useful in the Islamic society. Tomorrow this idle talker could move his lips all he wanted; with his shrewd parables he could needle the rigid and dogmatic doctors of law. And by God and His glory, Islam needed to be revived, needed to be ever watchful.

"Wait!" the general repeated. "Tell him . . . "

"He says: *Read! Read in the name of the water. There are springs and there are rivers. Some rivers never reach the sea, or dry out along the way. Others are born throughout the centuries, nourished with the water coming down from the springs. Boutr Aït Yafelman, you who are but a small river, ask the leader of the Muslims to whom you are transmitting my words if he still remembers his father."*

Something cracked in the immense structure his dreams had created with such tenacity and love. Tariq felt the echo within his bones. A single-minded man, where all the resources of his desire to succeed as well as the *will* to succeed fused in one idea, he was certain, knew for certain that the undertaking he had conceived for such a long time, would soon see daylight and spread over time and space. He had planned everything, from the mosque-cathedral to its future muezzin; from the hanging gardens to the army of gardeners, sons of Ispahan, Kairouan or the valley of the Moulouya who were already at the worksite—and the flower clock, down there on the hill which hundreds of arms were busy clearing right now; the libraries at the foot and within hearing of the public fountains; the maze of multicolored merchants' galleries, of the galleries of chased precious metals, of fruits of three continents; flights of birds trilling from the patios and terraces; patios bathed in light and serenity where people would take their meals accompanied by music and sharing them with strangers, the cripple, the orphan, anyone who would knock at the door and say: "I am a guest of God." Hands would use what they had created, joining the senses to their surroundings, combining art and daily life, joining the individual to the group in such a way as to make solitude disappear forever—the solitude of man, of a country, of a race, of a culture; the work of the body would not be stopped by borders nor fight with the work of the spirit. The unity would be so complete, so intimate, that all citizens of Andalusia, be they Muslims, Jews, Christians or atheists, would not wish to live in a different world, neither here on earth nor in the hereafter . . . Yes, he had been dreaming, loving, giving birth to all of it. Planned the future in its smallest details except one: the past.

Leaning over the ramparts, Boutr continued to translate painfully, as if each word was a tooth being pulled from his jaws.

"Does the leader of Islam remember his ancestors? They were not Muslims. Yet they gave him life. It is this very life that runs its course since the beginning of time."

Cupping his hands, Tariq suddenly yelled with all his strength:

"Ancestor of the Berber people, you are my guest. What is more, I am yours and am asking for your hospitality. I need a man like you, old and experienced, to remind me constantly of the importance of the past, if by bad luck I should get lost in utopia or barbarity. I well know that the past has devoured all of God's prophets and swallowed their messages. I well know that this old past from which Islam has risen as if from an abyss, has risen again, is more present than ever. All day long, my messengers report to me on the noise and the fury of bloody battles raging between the various staff officers of the Empire, from Damascus to this city here where no fewer than five emirs are established with all their vassals, while waiting for something better. . . . All of them are direct descendants of the Prophet, all of them are rivals. And you, here you are, at the cross-roads of destiny, you of whom I know nothing except the few silent words my lieutenant has spoken aloud to me and which leave a profound echo in my soul. That is why I beg you to help me, whether I dream or not, whether I am right or wrong, whether God inspires me or not."

Slowly, like a river subsides, the smile faded from Azwaw Aït Yafelman's face, all traces of kindness or good will disappeared. His face was no more than a lonely and desolate shore, a waxen mask furrowed with wrinkles. Only the lips were moving. Fascinated by this face alone, Boutr said slowly:

"*Time is long. I come and I go, when it sometimes precipitates itself and men stray from the path.*"

"Have I strayed from the path?" Tariq asked in great distress.

"*In the name of the father you did not know, in the name of the spring, in the name of the roots of the tree of life, listen: I have undertaken this march for a birth and for a death. Nothing distinguishes one from the other. One is imminent, in two or three hours time. The other . . .*"

"Well?"

"*Are you ready to face the future if I lift some of its veils for you?*"

"God alone knows the future and may He forgive me: I would call on the devil himself if need be. Go ahead. Lift as many veils as you can. I am ready."

Feverish and tensed like an arc over the ramparts, Boutr gathered the words and sentences he read on the old man's lips. He was ready to turn them into audible syllables, turning eagerly towards his chief, when suddenly he gasped. Very briefly. His face turned to stone.

"Well?" Tariq asked. "What's the matter with you?"

Boutr gasped a second time. He hid his eyes. With a voice so low it was barely audible, he said:

"The sun is blinding me. I can't see the features of the Master of the Hand."

"May it blind you for real. Talk. Every word."

"The master's lips move too quickly. I can't follow."

"Move your tongue just as fast. Word for word, without shortcuts or embellishments. Exactly what he is saying. Nothing else."

"You will kill me if I speak."

"I will kill you if you don't speak."

Boutr remained still, neither dead nor alive, for the space of a breath or for an eternity. His eyes darted from one to the other, rapidly, frightened, from the man of ancient times to the man of modern times, in a breathtaking gallop of History. When he opened his mouth, it was to stick out his tongue and bite it until it bled. And then, without hesitating even for one moment, he jumped over the wall into emptiness.

8

Tariq Bnou Ziyyad returned home by night fall. Throngs of admirers accompanied him all along the way: chiefs of clans asking the support of his army, job seekers who had nothing to offer but their arms and enthusiasm, recent converts who had converted at the eleventh hour and wanted an explanation of one verse of the Koran or a hadith of the Prophet, artists and scholars from all directions who were asking for an audience to show off their talents. He did not grant them a single word. To none of them. Not a look, not one sign that he noticed them. As soon as the door of his house opened, he slammed it in their faces.

Oum-Hakim received him in silence. She served him a broth made with the little white snails with a black circle in the middle that one could find among the rushes on the border of the river. They had simmered, without ever boiling, since early morning, seasoned with seventeen ingredients of equal strength and aroma. The result was a symphony of juices which had the power to reinvigorate the saddest hearts and to restore flagging virility.

Tariq drank three bowls of it in small sips. Then he went to lie down on his couch. Oum-Hakim took his sandals off and helped him undress. Her eyes wide open, she said:

"I would like to have your child, Lord and Master."

He looked at her for a long time. She did not flinch, but added in a whisper:

"I would like a child that has your weakness. That is what I have always loved in you: your weakness."

That night, she did not die from his passionate love-making, but almost. At daybreak, she knew that the dream of Tariq, son of Ziyyad and son of Islam was at last becoming reality: in her womb.

o o o

Two days later, Tariq Bnou Ziyyad was put in chains by order of his hierarchic superior, General Moussa ibn Noussaïr, governor of Ifri-qiyya. In the darkness of his jail, he had plenty of time to reflect upon the influence of Islam, both present and future. The man who had just clapped him in irons was a Muslim as he was, in heart and in words. Both of them worked with all their faith to establish the Kingdom of God. But why must this Kingdom, even before being born, devour its children, beginning with those who had cleared the path and laid the first stone? And if it was ever born, where would he find his place in this striving for power, in the contempt and the devaluation of human beings? Truly, the souls of the sons of Adam were as old as the world, old in its instincts, its passions, and even in its ideas.

What went on in the souls was permanent and independent of the march of History, Islam or no Islam.

"The day when certain signs will appear from your Lord, no soul will benefit from its faith" the Koran said.

Gesture for gesture, syllable for syllable, Tariq relived the last moments of his lieutenant, Boutr, down on the ramparts of the city. Perhaps Boutr had experienced a revelation of what awaited the Islamic community for which he had fought with all the Berber passion that lived inside him. And the moment he knew, he had ceased to know. He had preferred to seek death rather than bow to Destiny. Born an infidel, he had after all preferred to return to the state of unbeliever. What . . . what had the man with the camel, this demon surged from the past, told him?

"Who is there," Tariq cried out suddenly. *Bismillahi rahmani rahim!* Who is speaking?"

There was only silence around him. The silence of the grave. In him, there was the voice. Behind his eyes, he still had the very intense memory of Azwaw Aït Yafelman. The ancestor of the ancient people looked at him with a smile, slowly moved his lips as if speaking to a deaf man. What he was saying had no words, *no religion*—no hope nor disillusionment. Here it was: the meaning was clear, concrete, as firm as a rock. Unalterable, savage.

Savagely, Tariq Bnou Ziyyad began to grind his teeth, as if he were sharpening them on each other, ready to bite any adversity. He tried to plug his ears, but his arms were chained to the wall. He could not even kill himself, contrary to his faithful lieutenant.

The voice of the man without a tongue and without words was rising, tormenting him.

9

Squatting between the legs of the woman, Azwaw Aït Yafelman contemplated the woman's abdomen. The Koran said: "*We will show you something grave.*" Nature had always made its reassuring voice heard: "It is very simple." But words were words—as many faces of the same truth as there were human beings on this earth.

Saber at his throat, the emir Qaïs Abou Imran had received him with transports of joy. He was dressed in white robes and a white turban, surrounded by his Praetorian guard.

"Blessed be the trace of your steps, master! God prolong your life and give you His blessing. Master, oh master, she is the apple of my eye, she is my heart, my home. She is consumed by fever. It has been a week already that her time has come. The most famous doctors have come to examine her and the midwives are legion. Nothing helps, neither potions nor blood-letting nor the seeds of the fennel flower . . . and yet, the fennel flower is highly effective against any illness of the mind or body. All my money, all my jewels, my life even would not suffice to prove even one ounce of my thanks to you . . . "

With noble bearing, Azwaw had entered the palace, gone along a corridor filled with horses, then crossed a huge antechamber open to the sky where rainbow-coloured fountains intertwined to form chanting columns of water rising from two onyx basins to twice the height of a man. He paused for a moment on the immense esplanade strewn with large stones and blocks of marble, waved his hand over his shoulder. The camel that followed him immediately bent its knees with a soft bleating of relief. His finger pointed to the water bags, the lute, everything the camel carried on its back, and servants rushed to discharge the animal.

Craftsmen busy with their work. Cooks stoking the wood fire frying millet dumplings to a golden brown in hot olive oil. Barbers shaving only the neck and mustache of their clients, according to the latest fashion. With bare feet, women stomped in rhythm on bundles of dirty linen rubbed with ashes and loam. The trunks of saplings that would give off various kinds of scents were whitewashed and put into furrows of sand to keep them moist while waiting for the day they would stand up and blossom. And up there, on the roof, carpenters were building a balcony with ceders from the Atlas, sawing, fitting, singing. Their eyes lifted towards the sky as if to take heaven as a witness, a dozen muezzin apprentices turned and turned, chanting, modulating the call to prayer, sometimes hitting the palm of one hand with the fist of the other to accentuate the rhythm of the prayer. Sitting under a tent, scribes dipped their reed pens into a bottle of ink made out of burned wool, writing down carefully word by word what immigrants from Hedjaz related to them of the deeds and words of the Prophet, according to a genealogical chain of oral transmissions.

"I heard so-and-so say that so-and-so told him that this person had told him under oath that the Prophet had said: *None of you will be a Muslim if he does not desire for his brother what he desires for himself.* Authentic hadith, certified to agree with the letter and the spirit . . .

I heard so-and-so tell that so-and-so heard the Prophet say: *If you are not plagued by guilt feelings, well, do as you like!* Authentic hadith certified to agree with the letter and the spirit.

Longing for reassurance, the emir Qaïs Abou Imran's words gushed forth like a torrent. He kissed Azwaw's hands, embraced him, explained the circumstances to him talking nineteen to a dozen, tears in his eyes:

"I am a Moudarite from the tribe of the Moudar, one of those Bedouins in their original state who never had anything but the desert in which they were born. An arid desert from the beginning of time. No pastures, no livestock, no oasis for miles around. If they know eternity, it has the face of the never-changing elements. They know hunger as well as endurance and patience. In order to survive, they sometimes made a razzia on the prosperous cities such as Medina or Mecca. They were the ones who provided the Prophet with his first followers. Then all of a sudden, everything was given to them: riches, power, the whole world at their feet. So I, the son of misery, who not long ago ate scorpions and balls of camel hair, have by God's grace become governor of Cordoba, from one day to the next. What can I feel but pride and sometimes shocks of fear faced with the gigantic task entrusted to me? And my brothers from other tribes of the Arabic peninsula, what do they feel? They are as proud as I am, as afraid as I am. They are now responsible for the world. And we have only one book, a single one, the Koran. It is the very basis of our power, our knowledge of the ins and outs of everything. But I question myself, humbly and profoundly. Do you know what has permitted us to conquer all the peoples from the East to the West? Our ignorance. Yes, our ignorance of organized nations, full of knowledge and culture. And here we are, suddenly discovering the sense of History. This implies on our part a forced march towards knowledge of what we are and of our surroundings. Our archives were only poetry. At present we are confronted by humanity: we have to learn very quickly, do everything to perfection—all without losing one grain of our basic nature, the children of the desert we are. Do you think this is difficult? I tell you that you can guess the riches of him who receives you by the amount of ashes covering his cooking pots. I, who am used to mirages, I tell you this: whatever man imagines is superior to what he sees, for the imaginary is always larger than the tangible. I am telling you this: there is one exception, Cordoba. This city will be beyond anything one could imagine. It will be the capital of civilization, both of the Orient and the Occident. It is already so, day by day, the city takes shape and comes to life. Tomorrow, science, art and technology will converge here. The worksite you are looking at will become a hanging garden. There will be flowers and blooming shrubs from all over the world. And in the middle of this garden, exactly where you are standing now, the throne of the throne room will be erected. The men you see sitting here have crossed half of the earth to come and tell what they heard about the hadiths of the Prophet. Our scribes gather everything in writing. This is the beginning of our History and it must be universal. Of course the prophetic traditions will be closely examined. We have to verify how they were transmitted and check the honesty of those who transmit them in order to establish the authenticity of the hadiths which are the foundations of the behaviour of the believers. And this one here . . . and that one over there, all those you hear practicing the call to prayer will be the future muezzins of the mosques I will have built. And there will be a mosque-cathedral of a magnificence that will eclipse the very memory of the palace of king Solomon, who was obeyed by the spirits of heaven and earth. By God, it will be the House of God! In waves, in tight ranks, people will enter it and the light of the zenith combined with the water music will go straight to their hearts. They will weep with joy when they hear the divine words: *Peace, peace until morning cometh!* His back turned to the crowd, sitting in front of the alcove carved into the wall, the 'mihreb', the imam who will have led the prayers will salute the people to his right, then to his left, and then with a voice resounding with the emotions of the whole world, he will say: AL-FATIHA! THE OPENING! I so would like to see this day born. On that day, everything will be accomplished: the unfolding of the divine soul which lives in each of us, purity, beauty and goodness."

He cried bitter tears, for a long time, thin and pathetic.

He then blew his nose between his thumb and forefinger. He said:

"Misery is our misery and ephemeral are our bodies! It is God who has the strength."

He pulled a small vial of aloe perfume from the sleeve of his tunic and perfumed his beard and eyebrows. He said:

"Allah!"

He said, vulnerable in his distress:

"My wife is young and still beautiful for her forty-two years. God has willed that she still be fruitful at this age. But master, oh master, each time she had a child, it was stillborn. She has already lost seven and who will ensure the line of the descendants of the Abou Imran, *my* line? "

Azwaw Aït Yafelman looked at him attentively. His eyes showed this quiet irony with which one looks at subjects of supreme indifference. Qaïs Abou Imran read the answer to his hopes and fears in Azwa's eyes, it was an answer without words, as clear as a mountain source. He felt a sudden inner revolt and wanted this new life, his heir, immediately. Suddenly he felt his soul rise to his collarbone. He mumbled something and turned on his heels. Without understanding.

Princess Kawkeb-al-Gharb was waiting for her delivery on a canopy bed in a large, oblong room. She was dazed by fever, dressed in a ceremonial gown and slippers made of braided gold threads. At her bedside, a gathering of women were crying and talking, wringing their hands as if it were they who were going to give birth in hellish

105

pain. Here and there slaves burned incense over the braziers: storax, sandarac gum, frankincense. Azwaw Aït Yafelman stood in the doorway and waited ten seconds, his arms crossed, for everyone to leave. Before closing the double doors and undressing the woman in labor, he indicated with short, precise gestures what he wanted done right away: they were to bring him his lute and water bags, and without making the slightest noise, everything was to be taken out of the room, the bed, braziers, furniture, rugs, everything down to the last trifle.

And now, sitting on his heels between the woman's thighs in the position of the *qâbil* (the one who receives the new-born child), he examined each detail of the body lying on the floor, bathed in perspiration. If he meditated on the overall signs, it was with the sensual meditation of the animal past of the human race. The closed lids were fluttering, the aorta in the neck pulsing. Her lips were dry, her teeth clenched. The veins of her legs, her belly, her breasts were light grey. The areolas around her nipples were brown and swollen. The swollen vulva was as tight as an oyster. The navel was protruding. Her respiration changed from a long, whistling breath to short gasps. Unsteady too were the waves of pain that raised the skin, but never in the same place, while she made small sounds, half-way between a cry and a low groan. Azwaw perceived all these symptoms with his most noble organ, his sight. Examining what he has observed and still wants to explore, he uses his middle finger and his ring finger jointly to touch the ankle, the forehead, the groin. Then, very quickly, he traces the high-placed uterus from the pubis to the sternum. From what he can feel and imagine, he knows at once that someone is in mortal danger, perhaps this woman, perhaps the child she carries in her womb, perhaps both of them. Both are fighting to live, one against the other.

Not one single time does Azwaw Aït Yafelman flinch. He continues to look at her calmly, without wavering—until the body of Kawkeb-al-Gharb suddenly disappears from his sight. And then a veil like a cloud appears between his eyes and what he was looking at just a moment ago. Images appear of what he has seen. He feels them enter him in an atom of time, sending his blood pulsing through his veins as in a gallop. Shivering, he realizes what his hands are about to do—these very old hands who are nothing but wrinkles and knots now. They are all he has left.

The lute is hanging on his back. He very gently lets it slide over his left shoulder onto his lap, as if it were a sleeping child. He softly touches the cords as if to wake them up, and then he lets its voice rise fully. The instrument becomes a living soul, as alive as the tree full of sap who long ago gave it its wood. Four cords made of cat gut, stretched to a breaking point. In the center, the fifth cord is made of braided horse hair, the bass. Beginning at the bass and coming back to it at regular intervals, to die there and to be born again, rises the voice of the Ancient Times, sensually musical, marking and beating like the changing of day to night, like the passing of the seasons, like the outpouring of desire, the flux and reflux of the sea, the rising flood of the river inundating the fields and plains, the rising flood of orgasm that submerges a women from the neck to the soles of her feet, the subsiding of the flood which leaves behind an earth covered with green and the daughter of the earth thirsty for more water, the bud of the flower when it opens for the first time, naked, discovering the splendid nudity of the earth, the unfurling winds of winter, the lightning of shooting stars in a summer night; the melodies of long ago are dancing, dancing and vibrating in uninterrupted waves pulsating without a beginning to eternity without end. Like this:

From far away, from the very depth of her childhood, through the fever and heavy semi-consciousness in which she is fighting, Kawkeb-al-Gharb only hears a vague accumulation of sounds which have neither sense nor center—nothing but a resounding appeal to the memory of her body. She opens her eyes. Immediately, Azwaw Aït Yafelman stops his playing. And then she perceives the message and understands, note for note. A terrible pain, rising from deep within her, tears her apart. She is back in the country where she was born, on the banks of the Oum-er-Bia. She is fourteen years old. Fourteen years of indescribable happiness, day after day, since the day she was born. With a full throat she is singing the song of the Mother of Spring:

"La-la-la-li-la-la-la-li-la . . ."

The water comes up to her knees, running and chanting through her legs spread wide apart. Before her, a white rock on which she beats the linens she has rubbed with wood ashes. Around her, in the rushes, pink flamingoes, not one of them moving. And in the air, above the middle of the river, countless flocks of birds. Sun. Peace. The sap boiling in her loins hardens the tips of her breasts, turns her eyes liquid.

"Yerma, hello, Yerma!"

Oh yes, she hears the bronze voice calling her from the other side of the river.

"Yerma! Hello, Yerma. I am coming over."

But she does not turn around.

"La-la-la-li-la-la-la-li-la . . ."

Behind her she hears the beat of the paddle, the creaking of the gliding boat, coming closer, closer . . . But still she does not turn around for the sheer pleasure of waiting for the waiting to end. "La-la-la-li-la-la . . . " In an instant everything will suddenly die, for someone very alive will jump onto the rock. Her father. As always, he will lift her up by the waist, spin her around and catch her in his arms. And her heart full of adoration for the past fourteen years, when she will open her eyes, the face of Azwaw . . .

With the voice of a child waking at dawn, Kawkeb-al-Gharb says:

"Azwaw!"

She breathes in short gasps. Whimpers. Repeats:

"Azwaw. Azwaw. You . . . you have come at last."

He smiles at her tenderly. And, at the same time, he howls. Wild, in a panic. Spits in his hands, rubs them one against the other. Immediately and sure of themselves, as if independent of his will, his hands begin to move, caressing, stroking the legs of the woman in slow, back and forth movements, ever-changing, stopping at the top of the thighs, just under the groin, where the muscles that would bring forth the child are located, kneading them. He does not touch the vulva, the flower of fire, beaded with dew—not yet. He knows that desire is born first, dies last. And that desire is really nothing but to become what we are essentially. He knows too that at the moment of delivery, the female reaches her supreme moment: she is at last herself. Alone, as in the beginning. Alone and free from everything she has been taught. Without culture, without human history, without religion. All of a sudden, evolution has disappeared, has never existed with regard to the child that will leave her womb, who fills her like a guest forced on her, a stranger, an unknown future she loves and fears at the same time. And this is how it is: this Islam he once heralded and chanted from the top of the minarets, Azwaw Aït Yafelman can still feel the waves of crushing pains when he had lived through it, felt it in a *feminine* way like a continuous giving birth, lasting for centuries. And this female here, sick or not, he had to deliver her without fail from her thoughts, if not from her adult beliefs, fears tensing up her body. He had to make her submit totally to the implacable laws of nature, not through her brain, but through her body, fibre by fibre. Make her go back in time and relive what she had been, a fetus in her mother's womb. He looks for the "chakwas", the two water bags made of goat's leather. He takes one, unties the string of hemp that closes it.

Water. It will be stale, no doubt. He has carried it for such a long time on the back of his camel, watching over it as if it were the apple of his eye. But the water comes from the Mother of Spring, the eternal river. He pours some out into his hand as into a shell and makes

Yerma drink, forces her to drink. All females are as thirsty as if they were on fire when they are in labor. He pries her mouth open, floods her with water. Some of it runs off to her chest, her belly, her sex. Well, all the better! And what do the words matter with which she tries to express her feelings, or what she feels or thinks about having been reunited with her father at last. The little Berber girl Yerma Aït Yafelman she was from her birth to her marriageable age or the Princess Kawkeb-al-Gharb she became in the course of history. Those are only names, a label language puts on her, but these names are not her identity. Identity is what remains primordial throughout a life, to the last breath: the marrow of the bones, the flamboyant appetite of the organs, the spring beating in the breast, irrigating the human body with a multitude of red streams. Azwaw Aït Yafelman, the man of ancient times, hears the inner voices distinctly, interprets them and admits their full meaning—if he perceives anything from the outside, he does not want to be aware of it, does not want to listen to one word his daughter tells him, words gushing from her like a waterfall. He remains deaf to the accounts of her wanderings across the world while he pulls a horn-handled knife from his belt.

It is the knife he used to scale and clean the shad, the sciena and the halibut, quivering in heavy nets in the mouth of the Oum-er-Bia, the same blade he used to cut the throat of the bull, upright on his hindlegs in the prairie at the side of the hill, down there in Azemmour, a lifetime ago. Slowly and methodically he sharpens his knife on the tiles, pays particular attention to its point. And then, with the speed of a feline paw, he traces four incisions in one single motion, in the armpits, in the muscles behind the knees. He sucks the blood drops mixed with some strands of hair that taste of wood and yeast. He bites through the woman's cracked and swollen lower lip. He catches the blood running out with a hard, tight mouth, drinks it. Hot. These blood drops he sucks from the primary zones of her body, will relieve the waves of pain hammering in her head, will cool the boiling kettle within her belly—stimulate her, prepare her for the ultimate joy: that which will grow from her womb without the pleasure given by any man and will transform, in one short moment, all pain into joy, the joy of creation.

Swiftly and precisely he arranges everything he will need within reach: leather pouches containing dried plants he collected, dried and ground years ahead, planning for this birth. He opens one of them, powders the scars he has made, mixes agrimony with shepherd's knot, white and purple spiked nettles. His left hand slides under Yerma's thighs, massaging and kneading them with all his strength. He massages and kneads the small of her back, her hips, her sides, without respite, while his right hand searches the corn-colored pubis, gently uncovering the hair, separating, unfolding, spreading the labia. Then, his fingers joined, he plunges into the vagina. At the same time, Azwaw bends forward and, with the tip of his chin, hammers the pubis like a door knocker, at the spot where the symphysis will soon separate into two bones to free the passage. When he reaches the mouth of the uterus, he caresses it, feels it dilating. Slowly he spreads his fingers and turns his hand completely. Is it Yerma who gives this terrible cry? It is so much like the one he gave earlier that it seems like a late echo. The hand closes up and pulls out with a splashing sound. At once Azwa's mouth follows and blows into her sex with all the strength of his lungs, then sucks, sucks with the centrifugal force of a suction cup. And it is *orally* that he feels the blessed contractions begin. Now he has to act fast, outdistance time. His face is bathed in sweat and tears. I want life! *Bismillahi arrahmani arrahim!* I want life! Life! LIFE! Death does not exist . . .

A civilized woman of the eighth century, the honored wife of the governor of Cordoba, Kawkeb-Al-Gharb is content to only look, suffer, submit, while her nature, as old as the world, obeys its own laws. And these laws are revealed to her, imposed on her by the old prehistoric man inspired by an iron will, gifted with a thousand flying hands, who arches her back, straddles her neck, makes her forehead touch the ground, unbends her like a hazel twig, loosens her up, softens her muscles, puts her in a crouching position, her knees fitting into her armpits, sits cross-legged between her open thighs, caresses her, kneads and smooths her skin wherever knots remain, sucks on her nipples. Suddenly she knows he loves her with a love of rock and fire—and because he loves her, he asks, demands, only a very simple, elementary thing of her: to stop thinking so action can begin. She lets herself be submerged by the goodness of his strength. Time goes backwards; forty-two years recede as if nothing, absolutely nothing important had happened since her birth. Someone told her: "Be!" And suddenly, without being aware of it, she begins to move. She follows, sometimes precedes, starts to control and to direct the spasms now closer and closer together. Soft and firm like a man's member, a forefinger breaks the water sack.

From that moment on, everything she saw and heard was forever engraved in her memory, never to be forgotten. His mouth without a tongue wide open, the ancestor of the ancient people *spoke*. He spoke, chanted, gave instructions down to the slightest detail. He did not address himself to her, who for him was no longer but a receptacle, a pregnant female whose time had come. No, he did not speak to her. Through imitating sounds, sometimes articulating them, through cries rolling in his mouth like rocks rolling in mountain gorges, he guided the child through the black tunnel—and the child responded to him, Azwaw could see it clearly, it was as if it threw back the blankets that had held him prisoner in a nine-months-long sleep. Shivering, tense and pathetic, dancing with his feet joint, clapping his hands, Azwaw Aït Yafelman shouted. In his voice he put his entire life, nearly a century of patience and tenacity. He gathered all the mornings which had found him still alive and offered them to this child, who was blindly feeling his way. He encouraged him in his first efforts, called to him, told him he was waiting for him, that he would not die before having seen him because he had to pass on to him something essential to ensure the survival of his people. He showed him the way that lead to daylight, gave him the order to turn, to try and struggle, more, more! . . . not to look back or he would drown in his mother's blood or come out of her womb feet first.

He came out head first, his fists clenched as if he possessed the world. A strong, male child, hairy, almost without a neck, his face almost as wrinkled as that of the centenarian who received him in his hands. Furious and terribly hungry. Azwaw Aït Yafelman understood him at once, just by hearing the child's wailing, full of vigour and fury, summing up a whole future destiny. He recognized the character as tenacious as crab grass which was the prerogative of his race. Trembling with pride, he recognized himself such as he had been all his life, in all circumstances. He said:

"Oho!"

He shook his head and repeated:

"Oho!"

No, not right away. Let's have a little patience, what the devil! He held him up by his ankles to clear his chest from mucus and cut the umbilical cord four fingers from the navel, cauterized the wound. He put him, red with hunger, on his mother's breasts where he began to wail again with all his might. Azwaw then returned to Yerma, caressing her hair, her forehead, her temples with infinite gentleness. She had not lost a limb, but he knew well that she felt as if she had been amputated. He gently massaged the constrictor muscles to ease out the afterbirth. Only then did he get back to the child. He anointed its limbs, oiled its palate to make the uvula come up, blew in its nose to clear the passages to the brain, made him gargle to prevent the intestines from blocking and their walls to stick to- gether. He spread a healing powder over the small body. And then . . .

And then, he opened the second water bag, gave him his fill to drink, directly, mouth to mouth. Finally he let him have the water bag, put it where his voracious appetite could reach it. He rose and went towards the door. He also left his camel and the camel colt. Let him eat them alive, if he was that hungry!

With the point of his knife, he traced an Arabic name in Arabic script on the door panel: "Mohammed." Like a seal. For centuries he had increased his doubts profoundly before admitting the depth of his belief. Just as he had fought truth—in order to know it. He could not go any further. His task was accomplished.

10

They named him Mohammed after the Prophet, which did nothing to calm his ravenous appetite. On the morning of the third day, Kawkeb-Al-Gharb's milk flowed in her breasts and she cried with happiness. It was a normal flow of milk for a normal child. And then, very quickly, her breasts became chapped and painful. She tried to heal them by putting the feedings further apart. Her milk dried up.

The palace cooks concocted some nourishment to strengthen her, a dish especially reserved for woman in childbed called *sellou* which kept the most dedicated faster satisfied from sun-up to sun-down during the month of Ramadan. It was made of ground roasted wheat, blanched almonds fried in argan oil and ground in a mortar, sesame seeds, cinnamon, green anise and honey. They made her *tajines mrouziyya*: saddle and tail of a ram simmered a long time with grated onions, green almonds, raisins, salted butter cooked a year ago, honey from the Atlas that tasted of cedar, without counting the white ginger, saffron flowers and the seventeen spices and ingredients, including cantharis, that make up this culinary jewel, *ras-al-hanout*. All day long, they made her drink almond milk. Nothing helped. There was not another drop of milk.

Finally, in desperation, they entrusted the perpetual howler to a bosomy wet nurse, a "drawiyya" whose original home was in the south of the Maghreb, at the borders of the Sahara. A second nurse was added for good measure, a Spanish captive who had recently embraced Islam for the love of love-making more than for divine grace or reasoning. This "suction pump with a child's head", as the servants called him (but one that never backed up, not even a burp), at present had four soft, sweet wells at his command, from which flowed as much of the white nectar of life as he wanted. At night, Mohammed slept between the two women, as blissfully happy as a mentally deficient. He grew stronger every day and rapidly regained the weight he had lost with such suffering during the first days of his life.

His mother often came to see him. Her visits became more and more frequent. Actually she came day and night, at any moment. Slowly, without noticing it, she could no longer sleep. She would sit down on a divan and take the child into her arms. At least, she tried. For as soon as he saw his mother, as soon as he felt her near him, he began to cry and fight until his face turned purple. His back and limbs became stiff and he acted as if possessed. It broke her heart.

"Let him be," her husband told her one night. He rarely came to the women's quarters. "Let him be, for the love of God. He is still a little animal."

She felt his sensible words like a command. She looked at her lord and master without any expression in her eyes. Where were the love songs he had composed for her that had set her on fire? It was true, she was no longer of use to anyone. Neither to him nor to the flesh of his flesh.

"He will come back to you one day, you know," he added. "Be patient, my angel, be patient with all your soul!"

These words of comfort and tenderness did not calm the pain within her. To the contrary. One day . . . which day? But it is now, now that I need my child and that he needs me . . . I would give him my blood instead of milk . . . be patient, haha! patient. But I have been patient for the last forty-two years. She watched him rock the baby on his knees, watched him caress him; she saw his little body relax, melting like butter, smiling his first smile. She ran out of the room, roamed from room to room, scratching the walls until her nails bled, tore out her hair. She collapsed from grief, at the end of her rope.

When she awoke, her bed was surrounded. There were a dozen doctors of law, among the most famous of the city. They took turns explaining to her the order of the world the Sublime Creator had established, the letter and its spirit. They explained to her the meaning of certain verses of the Koran pertaining to life. They reminded her that the Prophet himself had not been nursed by his mother, which hardly had kept him from fulfilling the tasks that you know, my daughter. Islam is confidence. Trust in God, glory be to Him.

If she listened to them until the end, it was with great pleasure, the rapt attention of a sincere believer, but she did not understand. What they told her easily entered her head, each of their words found its exact place there. But not one of them *penetrated*. Perhaps she was only a Muslim in her head but not in her body. As long as this spiritual session lasted, she remained polite, but unable to give an adult answer. How could her lips express her child's feelings? She just smiled. The holy men blessed her, herself, her husband, her son and future children, *incha Allah!* And they left her, satisfied with themselves and their knowledge.

That night she slept soundly, which had not happened to her for a long time. The very next morning and all through the following week, she was taken with a frenetic desire to wash. Everything seemed dirty to her, beginning with her hair. She washed it with *ghasoul*, a paste of loam, a decoction made of cloves and rinsed it abundantly with clear water. She then washed her feet, her hands, her clothes, the bed linens of her room, the walls and all the corners. Everything was dirty with shame and sin. She gathered her army of servants and slaves and led them a terrible life. There was not a speck of dust left in all of the palace, not a trace of smoke or grease on the cooking utensils.

This period of excessive activities which had channelled her thoughts was followed by inertia. Solitude seized hold of her, isolated her from those around her, kept her intensely distrustful. Why was everyone spying on her? Why were all these ears listening to every word she spoke? And if she broke out in laughter in the midst of a *zikr* or a *samaa*, why did everyone look at her in consternation, why did someone immediately put an arm around her shoulder, an arm full of pity and commiseration? And why, especially why did they tell her in a whisper to keep quiet? Oh no, she could no longer keep quiet. She did not say anything wrong. She was happy. She was sure. The door will open . . . Azwaw will enter, take her into his arms, know her and fill her with his semen as he had long ago. He is there, swimming in the Oum-er-Bia, swimming with her between two waters while his member quivers in her and lifts her up . . . He can do anything, my father. He is the Master of the Hand. He will make me become small again, very small . . . He will inundate me with his milk . . . and . . . his milk will flow in my breasts . . .

o o o

They put her on a desert mare and with an escort, made her ride full speed across the distance that separated Cordoba from the straits of Gibraltar. There they tied her to a boat. The boat was fastened to a cable. The sea was stormy. According to the famous specialist for mental diseases, Doctor Zwitten Baba Abderrahim, this was the treatment the princess needed. The rolling of the waves and the pitching of the boat would make her vomit everything from her very depths, even the dizzyness that had confused everything in her head. It was an excellent treatment.

After one day and one night, the boat was hauled in. Kawkeb-Al-Gharb was calm, very calm, as still as a corpse. But she did not die until a few seasons later, nobody ever knew what she died of nor in what circumstances. The emir Qaïs Abou Imran was the first magistrate of the city and, as such, was entitled to certain considerations. He had the Prayer of the Absent recited over her body which was then buried in the cemetery of the martyrs, near the south gate, Bab-al-Mandab. After all, it was no more than justice. Had she not given him a son? The heritage of the Abou Imran was ensured, glory be to God!

In that he was right and wrong at the same time.

o o o

On the same day, Azwaw Aït Yafelman walked into the Oum-er-Bia, almost at the same moment when the first shovels of Andalusian soil fell, to the rhythm of grave voices chanting the canticle of the dead, on the body of his daughter. The rising sun turned the surface of the river into a blazing fire, made the rushes come alive, gay and glittering, while legions of sea gulls flew eternally between the sky and the earth. The concert of the birds greeted him from miles around.

Setting one foot in front of the other, the ancestor of the ancient people started to go down to the depth of the river bed, to the place where the boiling waters of the Mother of Spring merge with the water of the ocean as in an act of love, in a roaring abyss. He could swim better than any fish in the world—but he made not one gesture to save himself. He had never asked for anything from anyone. He could ask for nothing more than what he had received during his long, very long life. And he did not want anymore. He had been given all that a man could desire—he knew that. He also knew that perhaps he would never have more.

When he arrived in the middle of the abyss, he let himself roll like a rock. His mouth open. The water of the eternal river filled his mouth, flooded his lungs, took away his last doubts. Contrary to the adults who leave this world with open hands, he, Azwaw Aït Yafelman, died with clenched fists, like a new-born child. He was still clutching the world.

o o o

Despite all the evident signs of a sanguine and domineering character, Mohammed Abou Imran was an easy child to raise, as docile as a lamb. The first months of his life were serene. All he asked was to eat and sleep. He walked early, talked quite late, and was not really interested in the songs, the fairy tales and legends of his nurses. To all the games they proposed to him, he vastly preferred exploring his genitals. Therefore they dressed him in confining garments day and night, and when they bathed him, they did it with lightning speed. It was not that in those days Islam veiled or reprimanded the manifestations of the body, but because the emir Qaïs Abou Imran intended to develop the brains of his heir as best he could, nourish it at the intellectual and ethic springs of the new civilization. One would have sworn that the child listened gravely to his father, that he drank in his words. He was very attached to him.

As the child grew older, his personality emerged. His features were heavy. He was an average adolescent who did not behave very well. Then he became an adult, strong but rather ordinary who showed no zest for life or the fire of dreams. Not an atom of what had made his maternal grandfather, Azwaw Aït Yafelman, a great man. Not one iota of the gigantic desire of which his mother had died. Nothing that came anywhere close to the vast human enterprise his father, the governor of Cordoba, was building. (Emir Qaïs did not remain governor for long. He firmly believed in his destiny, in the glorious future of his issue. Like most of the fervent servants of Islam—and the previous religions—he was nothing but a straw in the hands of God. The winds of History blew on him, made him dance, finally swept him away, him, his family and his vassals. Alliances and broken alliances followed each other with dizzying speed. Qaïs only prepared the coming of the dynasty of the Omeyyads of Spain. A long time later, one could still find Abou Imrans among the most illustrious families of Fès, in the Maghreb . . .)

No, Mohammed Abou Imran did not shine with intelligence. He did not leave his seal on his era. But, when he became of age, he took his place in History. On his wedding day, to be exact. He was not aware of it, and it was beyond the comprehension of his contemporaries. To guess what was going to happen, they would have had to live for several centuries. The wife fate, aided by the arrangements between tribes, had placed into Mohammed's arms was named Jawal . . . a natural child born to General Tariq Bnou Ziyyad and an impure captive, Oum-Hakim. At present, the memory of Spain's conqueror was honored. They built mausoleums for him. Streets were named after him: *Chariaa Tariq ibn Ziyyad*. Beyond actions and words, Azwa's blood continued to beat and bear fruit. The ova opened up and captured the spermatozoon from generation to generation. Through uncountable hidden ramifications in space and time, Azwaw Aït Yafelman's life was reborn. And with him was reborn the Islam of the early days, bare and foreign amidst the pomp of the Arabic civilization at its zenith. It happened in a Berber village in the Atlas, at the beginning of the eleventh century. His name was Abdallah ibn Yassin.

11

"Enter, stranger, enter in peace. The first day of eternity has arrived."

With these words from the Koran the stranger was received at the south gate of Cordoba, on a bright morning in the year of Christian grace one thousand fifty four. He was dressed in a burnous woven of brown wool and wore a goatskin hat. He was long and lean like an ox tail. He did not have to give his name nor tell them where he came from. He was taciturn. Furthermore, no one asked him any question. The fact that he was not a citizen of Cordoba was enough, made him at once into an honored guest. Any son of Adam who lived outside of the ramparts of Cordoba—perhaps even outside of the Andalusian borders—could only be from an underdeveloped country. They were going to show him paradise.

"Drink, brother. It is only pure dew hundreds of gardeners have collected at dawn from flower petals, drop by drop, in one or two of our hundreds of gardens. The hands of maidens in the bloom of youth threw some grains of gum arabic on glowing braziers. When the grains began to smoke, they placed an earthenware jug upside down on the brazier to let the scent of the gum permeate the jug. Only then did they pour in the dew drops. Here is the jug, stranger. Drink and may the beauty of the world descend into you!"

He drank. It was delicious, refreshing. He did not speak.

"And eat. It is *herbel*, a snack while we wait for breakfast. It is only coarse wheat ground in a mortar. Of course, the women have sorted it grain by grain. Yes, they gather in neighborhood groups, sometimes it is the neighborhood of the carpenters', another time the weavers', sometimes the perfume-makers' turn. And so you are sustained by all the people, the whole community. So, they have washed the wheat and cleaned off the hulls. They started last night. It takes time to prepare the good things in life. They covered the *herbel* with rainwater, then placed it over a wood fire. It cooked all night and nobody had to watch it. One must never touch it while it rises and cooks. This morning they stirred it with a lemon wood spoon. They boiled milk fresh from the cow and slowly poured it on the wheat, stirring all the time. One woman added salt, another one sugar, a third fresh butter and orange-flower water. Those three are specialists, they are called the 'tasters'. Yes, they are six to seven months pregnant. As you know, at this stage of their pregnancy their palate is the most sensitive. There are always pregnant women in our city. They taste and adjust the seasoning of all dishes in all of our homes. So when their time comes, they give birth to splendid children. Taste, stranger. And may you bathe in the blessings of Allah."

He tasted. It was succulent. He did not say one word, took another spoonful, and another, and yet another . . . One would have said grains of honey with the tang of the soil, soft and at the same time crunchy under the teeth. They had brought him to the guard house accompanied by music. They had sat him on a brocaded sofa, placed silver edged embroidered cushions in his back. Under his feet, on the walls, a symphony of carpets and wall hangings where azure, indigo, parma green blended into a dark-red background. *Qanoun*, bass violin, *oud, derbouka*, the quartet sat in a circle, played and sang in unison the "mouwachahat', this Andalusian music that filled the guest with physical well-being, stimulated his appetite and then helped him to digest.

Afterwards, they led the stranger (he was still silent) to the adjoining bathing chamber. Like two vibrant springs, hot and cold water flowed into glazed earthenware shells, one from the mouth of a bronze lion, the other from the beak of a ceramic cormorant bird. The man who had just eaten took the cake of soap they held out to him. It was shaped like a mons veneris. He smelled its rose perfume, thoroughly washed his hands and rinsed his mouth. They sprayed his bald head and his beard with musk, slipped a ceremonial robe of Yemen silk over his burnous and shod his feet in slippers so soft and so immaculate the stranger was startled. He had never walked on anything but the rough soles of his feet. Until nightfall, as long as the visit of the city lasted, the stranger remained the same, his face austere without any expression, not even in his eyes. A witness from another planet.

There was an uninterrupted succession of fountains, water music, laughter of the slow-moving crowd, an orchestra at every street corner, a huge display of copper, gold, mint, fine cloth and fine-crafted goods. It was the first merchants' gallery with finely wrought screens and balconies, skeins of wool and silks stretched overhead like a canopy from one facade to another in a riot of warm colors. The light of the midday sun fell through this canopy and split into a spectrum of primary colors that became a blaze of complementary colors. The man they led by the hand to show him civilization tried in vain to jump over the rays of green, ochre, cobalt, yellow, emerald and ruby . . . he did not want to spoil them.

Balek! Make way, make way for the stranger! . . . *Balek!*

"Eighty-thousand stores. Look."

He saw it well, noted everything, had no comments.

From each store, a merchant came forward with a smile to meet the stranger, an offering in the palm of his hands.

"Take it, brother. It is a sample. You are my guest."

"Here, brother. Smell this grape before you taste it."

"My guest . . . brother . . . guest . . . take . . . it's a gift . . . "

"Make way, make way! *Balek!*"

The man with the sad face tasted a date, another date, a few grapes, a round peach, a purple olive—one of those *meslalla* which had been marinated in its own juice and which tasted like a clitoris. He chewed carefully. The seeds and stones he put into the hood of his burnous.

"Come," the captain of the guard, who was acting as a chamberlain, told him. "Follow me. And may your soul prostrate itself before what your eyes will behold."

Majestically, the stony-faced man entered the second merchants' gallery and crossed it very slowly. Here it was neither wool nor silk that formed the canopy, but a hanging garden. From the porch of each house flowering branches grew along the vestibule, passed through an opening made in the door frame for this purpose, climbed up the front of the house, surrounded all the windows with tiaras of flowers. Their living sprays of blossoms fell two-men's heights to form a dazzling cupola. White and purple jasmine, roses, bitter orange blossoms, *elranj*, hollyhocks, bougainvilleas, sun stars and many other scented blossoms for which they did not yet have an Arabic name. From the street, paved with glazed brick gleaming with emerald green, water fountains rose: their liquid rays, chanting note for note a whole range of melodies, never touched the flowers, not even with one drop, but stopped short about the width of a man's hand. Just enough to refresh them with a soft breeze.

The stalls were not next to the houses, but in the middle of the street, standing next to one another, made of wood and built round like kiosks. This is where the master craftsmen of the perfume makers worked. They had all the essences right there. People brought their food and drink to them. From morning to night, sometimes throughout the whole night, they were bent over their *quettara*, fervently watching how the fragrant essence fell drop by drop from the flower petals. And each one of them made it a point of honor to put a tiny drop of their product on the stranger who, albeit unwillingly, allowed them to put it on his forehead, between his fingers, to his earlobes.

"And now," his mentor told him, "come and feast your soul on the brilliance of our science. Enter and listen."

There were tiers, rows of seats arranged in tiers all the way to the sculpted ceiling from which rock crystal chandeliers were suspended. Sitting cross-legged on a rostrum, the professor of medicine gave his magistral course to students who had come from the four corners of the world.

. . . "One day I counted forty different vegetables and meats to create one single dish. I did say: forty. But let us get back to our subject. Medicine is a science which includes everything, because its purpose is the health of the human body, life. The physician tries to maintain the good health of those who seek him out. He also tries to prevent illness. He first identifies the trouble, not forgetting the patient's psychological problems, then he gives his diagnosis. He also chooses the form of treatment, judging the effectiveness of a remedy by its composition and its virtues. He evaluates the progress of an illness and the patient's tolerance of a medication by examining the urine and the stool of the sick person and checking his pulse. In this he imitates nature and he tries to give it support, in other words, he encourages the patient's will to live . . ."

He spoke for a long time, explained the phenomenon of the blood flowing in the arteries, blood circulation, circulation in the lungs. Like a leitmotif, he always came back to the essential point in medicine: the relationship patient-illness-environment. If he understood and remembered, the stranger did not let it be evident. He was even sparing of his spittle.

They led him to the college of music. It was in the midst of a park planted with fragrant trees. Each student, from his earliest age on, first had to build the instrument of his choice, work on it, raise it like a child, nourish it with patience and love, learn its texture grain by grain, its feel, its smell—its personality. Sometimes this took years. And when the student finally played his first note, he was less a master of the instrument than a lover at the feet of his beloved, listening to her, or like a Bedouin, blood brother of his horse. The stranger's eyes embraced everything carefully. He listened for a long time to the joyous tunes and the detailed explanations of the teachers. He did not make one sound.

They invited him to dinner in a private home, a small palace. A man entered. He turned around when he noticed the one who was certainly not a Cordovan. His hand held out, he said:

"Come share our meal. You would honor us. After you, brother. This house is your house."

They rolled four round tables before the brother which richly dressed servants loaded with steaming dishes. He gorged himself, but without heaving one sigh of content or showing any emotion whatsoever. They washed his hands in a tiered silver basin. The tiers had been cleverly perforated like the sound holes of a lute. When the servant poured water from a kettle, the water falling through the holes became a chant of strings. It had been a gala occasion, the afternoon was almost over. So they invited the stranger to lie down for a little rest while awaiting the festivities in the caliph's palace. He opened his mouth, said:

"No."

He stood up and asked in a grave voice:

"Where is God?"

The captain of the guards immediately became suspicious. He asked the question which had been burning on his lips since morning:

"Who are you?"

"A Berber from down there."

"Where is that?"

"Sidjilmassa."

"What's that?"

"Nothing. The Atlas."

"What is your name?"

"Abdallah. Abdallah ibn Yassin."

"What do you do for a living, Abdallah?"

"Nothing. I pray."

The officer suddenly broke into happy laughter.

"You are a *fqi*? You teach the Koran to the Barbarians?"

"I am a marabou."

"You want to visit our mosque-cathedral, the mosque of the Omeyyads?"

"That is why I came all the way from the mountain. For no other reason."

"Come, man of God. Follow me. *Balek! Balek!* . . . Make way, make way. Make way for the man of God. Notice to the population: this man here will lead the prayers . . . *Balek! Balek!*"

Behind them, the crowd assembled like waves, grew larger and followed like a procession. A new imam, even for one day, was always welcome.

Abdallah ibn Yassin took his shoes off, shed the robe they had given to him as if it were a winding sheet, performed his ablutions in the basin of the mosque, one of the countless basins in the orange-tree court. He scrubbed himself vigorously. He felt impure from all the luxury that embalmed him like a corpse. He used a lot of water. Then, slowly, he crossed the forest of pillars.

The "mihreb" was in marble, so smooth and polished that it amplified and echoed the sound for miles around, filled with the four echoes of the mosque and the resonance of the vaulted ceiling. Abdallah went there, turning his back to the faithful. For years and years he had waited for this moment—he, a believer as solid as his native mountain. *"Thabaraka alladi biyadihi al-moulk . . . Glory to him in whose hands lies the kingdom! . . . He who created death and life to make of you, yes of you, His best creation . . . "* The sura beginning with these words was the one he liked best of all. It was simple and beautiful, for it summed up Destiny.

And this is how Destiny manifested itself: Abdallah had already opened his mouth, wanted to bring up from his throat all the voices of all of his ancestors whose lives and deaths were in his blood, generations after generations, drop for drop, and their sweat and tears, their faith and disillusionment—and then . . . And then the Voice suddenly resounded in his body, reached his brain, lamed his tongue. Distinctly and clear the Voice said:

"Do not recite. Not one word. This is My command. Leave this place and act according to My voice."

He left and acted. Three seasons later, in the year one thousand fifty-five, he built strongholds at the head of his commandos, conquered the Maghreb and the larger part of Spain, founded the Berber dynasty of the Almoravids which was to last nearly a century—the space of a renewal, an infinitesimal spring of sidereal eternity.

> *Dreamed in the Middle Ages on the vestiges of a birth, in Cordoba, then in Fès; written in France 1984-1985, at night, sometimes in the afternoon, while my youngest child TARIQ was sleeping.*

Glossary

Afrith	Demon
Allah Akbar	God is great
Almoravids	Berber dynasty reigning over Morocco and Muslim Spain, founded by Abd Alklah ibn Yassin (1055–1147).
Askandaria	Arabic name for Alexandria
Balek	Take care
Baraka	Allah's blessings
Bendir	A drum fashioned from a goatskin stretched over a round wooden frame.
Burnous	Long, loose cloak worn with a hood, traditionally worn by Arabs and Moors.
Cadi	Muslim judge
Derboulka	Musical instrument
Djellaba	A loose-fitting garment with a hood, worn traditionally by men, but now worn by women as well.
Fqi	In Islam, an expert on religious knowledge.
Guinmbri	A musical instrument
Hadith	Sayings attributed to the Prophet.
Incha Allah	God willing
Ifriqiyya	Ancient Arabic name for Tunisia and eastern Algeria.
Imazigen	Berbers
Majnoun	A person possessed by evil spirits, a mad person.
Marabou	An Islamic, often Sufi, holy man.
Medina	A native quarter of a North African city.
Mektoub	It is written
Omeyyads	Dynasty of Arabic caliphs who founded the Caliphat of Cordoba (756–1031).

Birth at Dawn

Oud	Musical instrument
Quanoun	Musical instrument
Roh	Go. Get out.
Samaa	Litany during which one hears the responses to invocations or music
Sherif	A noble descended from the Prophet
Souk	Marketplace, often stalls in covered streets.
Wallah	I swear
Youyous	Undulations, usually made by women to express emotion or encouragement.
Zaka	The offering each Muslim must give to the poor.
Zikr	Litany for one or several voices.

Birth at Dawn, the third volume of Chraibi's tetralogy, deals with the arrival of Islam with the all-conquering Berber-Arab armies in the 8th century (Christian chronology), just before the conquest of Cordoba and Andalusia.

Aït Yafelman (protagonist in the other volumes of the tetralogy) is now in his tenth decade, figuring prominently, if mysteriously, in the role of mage, doctor, and fiery soul of the Berber people, as Islamic ideals sour into greed and bloodlust.

Considered a Francophile because of his once warm acceptance of French education and culture, Chraibi (born in El Jadida, Morocco in 1926), early on supported French colonial rule, but soon became as critical of the entire Occidental world as he was of the Islamic world. Molded by both, Chraibi is sympathetic with neither. He practiced medicine for a few years but turned to writing in 1952. In 1956 he began work also in French radio and television.

Three Continents Press has published the first three volumes of the tetralogy as well as the English translations of three other works by Chraibi: *The Simple Past (Le Passé Simple)*, Chraibi's first novel, published in French in 1954, *The Butts (Les Boucs)* in 1983 and *Mother Comes of Age (La Civilisation, Ma Mère! . . .)* in 1984.

Note on Translator

Of German birth, Ann Woollcombe served in the German "Peace Corps" in the Cameroon in the 1960s, married a Canadian career diplomat and lived in Morocco during one of their "postings." She has been an official translator of French to English and vice-versa for the Canadian government and has translated two works from African literature for Three Continents: *Fary: Princess of Tiali* (1987) by Senegalese writer Nafissatou Diallo and *Mountains Forgotten by God* by the Moroccan novelist Brick Oussaïd (1989).